"I was asking whether or not you'd reached the point where you were opening yourself up to another relationship, and possibly, a family of your own," Amelia added.

Craig could pretend to himself that her question was of a personal nature. As in, asking because she was interested in the answer for herself. Like she might consider starting a relationship with him that could go someplace great. Someplace permanent.

He didn't make that mistake.

"I haven't met anyone who's inspired me to that extent," he told her. And went on to describe a couple of the women he'd dated over a period of months, each exclusively, during the past year. They'd both been open to more. As soon as he'd felt their growing affection, he'd felt compelled to break things off with them. "I'm not out to hurt anyone," he told Amelia, hoping that she understood that she was included in that statement.

Odd, but it was kind of nice talking to her. A woman who had no interest in him, and yet one with whom he held a deep connection—the child growing inside her.

* * *

THE PARENT PORTAL:
A place where miracles are made

D0047125

Dear Reader,

Welcome back to The Parent Portal! You get back-to-back visits here, with *The Baby Affair* this month and *Her Motherhood Wish* next month! The two stories are stand-alone. They only share a town, a clinic, not each other, and I poured my heart into both of them.

The Baby Affair was a special book to write. It's the story of a man and a woman who've never met suddenly being thrown together through concern for the life of their unborn child. And it's the story of two sisters who were so certain, after their childhood, that they'd never marry. And the story of how a life that hasn't even been born can change their worlds.

It's a story about love, in all its different dresses.

I particularly loved writing this book because I never had a sister and have always longed for one. And because, as I was writing it, I was awaiting news of the birth of my grandson. I'm thrilled to say he arrived happy, safe, sound and healthy!

I love to hear from my readers! You can find me at www.tarataylorquinn.com and follow me on social media, contact me, or sign up for my newsletter from there! See you next month!

Tara Taylor Quinn

A Baby Affair

Tara Taylor Quinn

HARLEQUIN
SPECIAL
EDITION

HARLEQUIN®
SPECIAL EDITION™

Recycling programs for this product may not exist in your area.

ISBN-13: 978-1-335-89444-1

A Baby Affair

Copyright © 2020 by TTQ Books LLC

All rights reserved. No part of this book may be used or reproduced in any manner whatsoever without written permission except in the case of brief quotations embodied in critical articles and reviews.

This is a work of fiction. Names, characters, places and incidents are either the product of the author's imagination or are used fictitiously. Any resemblance to actual persons, living or dead, businesses, companies, events or locales is entirely coincidental.

This edition published by arrangement with Harlequin Books S.A.

For questions and comments about the quality of this book, please contact us at CustomerService@Harlequin.com.

Harlequin Enterprises ULC
22 Adelaide St. West, 40th Floor
Toronto, Ontario M5H 4E3, Canada
www.Harlequin.com

Printed in U.S.A.

Having written over ninety novels, **Tara Taylor Quinn** is a *USA TODAY* bestselling author with more than seven million copies sold. She is known for delivering intense, emotional fiction. Tara is a past president of Romance Writers of America and is a seven-time RWA RITA® Award finalist. She has also appeared on TV across the country, including *CBS Sunday Morning*. She supports the National Domestic Violence Hotline. If you need help, please contact 1-800-799-7233.

Visit the Author Profile page
at Harlequin.com for more titles.

For Rachel. From the moment I knew you were growing inside me, you owned me. And you still do. I love you forever and beyond.

Chapter One

"Listen to your voicemail. Christine called from the Parent Portal. You need to call Dr. Craig Harmon. I left you a voicemail about it. And here's the doctor's number, so you don't have to write it down." A phone number ended her sister's frantic text.

Sitting in the window seat in a plane crowded with travelers facing customs, Amelia was weary from an eight-hour flight. She immediately put a protective hand over her mostly flat belly, tucking it beneath her tight white cotton shirt and lace-pocketed black jeggings. She warned herself to stay calm. Stress could have a negative impact on the baby.

So could all of the other people taking their time to vacate the plane. Because they were causing her stress. With a couple of thumb swipes she accessed voicemail. Pressed to listen.

"Amelia, lishquensenhse..."

It went on for thirty-three seconds, that garbled sound in Amelia's ear where her younger sister's message should have been. Either Angeline had been in a loud crowded place when she'd left the message, or technology had just failed. Either way she was screwed.

Hell. Just hell. Why did she need to call a doctor? Please God, let her baby be okay. At a little more than fourteen weeks along, she'd passed the critical first three months.

Standing, she hit her head on the rounded ceiling of the plane, attempting to see how much longer she was going to have to wait.

At least ten rows. Maybe eleven. She glared at the backs of slow-moving heads and pressed her sister's speed dial icon. And got Angeline's voicemail.

Of course.

Ripping a silent expletive that stood in for the frustrated tears she was holding back, Amelia remembered that Angeline, who was also her business partner, was in a meeting with the New York designer who could ensure their financial security for a long time to come. Not that they were hurting, anyway. Who'd have thought sewing lace on jean pockets, and adding lacy embellishments to their purses as teenagers, would have exploded into a retail business that kept them both bountiful?

Six rows to go. Voicemail still garbled the second time she tried to listen to her sister's message. She'd bumped her head on the low ceiling twice more. And the guy in the aisle seat at the end of her row hadn't bothered to put his tablet and extra battery back in the pack under the seat in front of him.

She had the number. At the rate things were going, she could have the call made and done before she exited her row. Action immediately followed the thought. Amelia was too het up to think twice.

For all she knew, Dr. Harmon was on staff at the Parent Portal, the private fertility clinic where she was being followed. Perhaps its staff just wanted to let her know he'd written an order for the sixteen-week ultrasound. Or some more blood work—there were a lot of things they could check on these days, and she'd opted for all of them.

As tired as she was, it would be like her to make

something out of nothing. And Angeline would think she'd heard the voicemail.

Taking comfort in the curtain of long auburn hair around her face, she stood slightly hunched, watched people slowly vacate and listened to the fifth ring—rehearsing words in her mind for when the receptionist picked up.

This is Amelia Grace. I was told to call this number... Is Dr. Harmon available?'

Three rows to go.

And a male voice answered her call.

"Craig Harmon…"

"Dr. Harmon?"

The call came in on his private line, where he was just Craig, but… "Yes."

"This is Amelia Grace. I was told to call you."

He'd been waiting hours for her call. But hadn't expected it would come that day. Maybe not even that week. Figured she'd need time to process.

He shrugged out of the white coat he still wore to see patients, where others of his peers opted for shirts and ties. White coats had pockets.

"Yes, thank you," he said, feeling anything but his usual confident self. He was generally the one offering calm reassurance. Assistance. Advice and treatment. He was the one with answers. Now *he* needed some. "As I told Ms. Elliott, at the clinic, I'd like for us to meet." He ran a hand through dark blond hair, which needed a cut. He had to do this.

"Excuse me?"

"Per the agreement," he said, and stood up from behind the massive cherrywood desk in his office at the clinic he owned along with six other doctors. He'd grown up in Sacramento, but a buddy of his from med school had first introduced him to Marie Cove, the little town south of LA, during med school, when he'd told him about a new fertility clinic there. What made it unique was the lines it left open between donor and client. The only way she'd have gotten his number was if the clinic had contacted her and told her that he'd requested to speak with her. That's how it worked. Either party could request at any time and the other party agreed to have at least a a conversation or other limited contact.

What he'd give now to have never heard of the place.

"What agreement?"

A hand in the pocket of his pants, Craig looked out toward the ocean beyond the cliff face across the street from his second-floor office and frowned. "With the Parent Portal."

"I'm sorry, who are you?" She grunted, as though she'd been shoved from behind. Or run into something.

"I'm the father of your child," he told her, getting more concerned by the second. More certain than ever that his need to connect with his biological offspring was valid.

Her lack of response added to his unease. "Ms. Grace, are you okay?"

"I'm…" She huffed. "Just getting off a flight from France. Can I call you back?"

Without giving him a chance to respond she hung up.

Leaving him with all of his questions, plus some, and no answers. He knew one thing more than he had previously, though.

His child wasn't even born yet and he or she was already a world traveler. He wasn't sure he liked that idea.

The father of your child. The father of your child? What the hell? Oh, God, what the hell?

Carrying a large black purse filled with the remainders of her snacks and a bottle of water, her tablet and her smaller purse crammed in there, too, Amelia made it down the narrow aisle of the aircraft and out to a crowded gate.

The father of your child. She made a quick bathroom stop. Washed her hands. Refused to look in the mirror. To risk seeing the panicked eyes gazing back at her.

Before hoisting her bag back up on her shoulder, she pulled out her phone and tried her sister again. Just in case Angeline was wearing her smart watch, saw the multiple notifications and chose to excuse herself from the meeting long enough to calm Amelia's heart rate.

They were in this together. After their own childhood—having a mother who loved them, but who had to answer to her husband first—they had both chosen to have their own families without marriage or partners. Amelia first, and then Angeline was going to have herself inseminated, too, down the road a bit. They'd agreed to be guardians to each other's child in the event anything happened to either one of them. They'd signed paperwork at the clinic, providing that they were both privy to any and all information. They even had each other's medical power of attorney.

Her younger sister didn't pick up.

Bag back on her shoulder, Amelia told herself she wasn't feeling nauseous, that this was not going to be the moment when she learned how morning sickness felt, and headed toward baggage claim.

Each step she took played a word in a recurring beat.

The father of your child. The father of your child. The father of your child.

He was wrong. This Craig Harmon guy who was posing as a doctor. Or even if he *was* a doctor, this information was still wrong.

Her child didn't have a father.

Her baby had come from a sperm donor, fulfilling a biological component.

Not a father.

Not. A. Father.

"You signed the paper, Mel." Angie's soft red curls drifted around her perfectly oval face as she faced Amelia. Her younger sister had arrived at their new corporate office space in Marie Cove at the same time as Amelia, who'd come straight from the airport. In a short denim skirt with lacy embellishments, a short-sleeved white cotton top and denim wedges, Angie looked ready to conquer the world, where Amelia, still in her travel-wrinkled jeggings and shirt, felt ready for a shower and bed.

After she took care of the business waiting on her desk.

Which would happen as soon as she could spare a brain cell to focus on it.

"I signed the paper for my baby's protection," she said now, holding back the frustration she felt toward her sister for something that wasn't at all Angie's fault. Her sister had expected her to hear the voicemail. And had known that Amelia would be all panicky and struggling to get the number from a fuzzy audio message, so she'd also sent the text.

She'd chosen the Parent Portal specifically because of the private facility's policy about openness of communication between biological components if the need ever arose. The biggest concern she'd had with an insemination was the black hole where paternal genetic history was concerned. Things that went beyond basic medical testing. Like a tendency toward obesity, or a history of obsessive compulsive disorder. The Parent Portal's personal database for each donor was much more extensive than a lot of clinics'. Not that she'd been seeking that kind of information, but if there was a problem, she could know that she could have all information to help make the best decisions…

"I never, in a million years, expected the donor to call me," she said, still standing. She needed to sit. Which was why she didn't. Giving in to weakness wasn't permitted in this kind of moment. She looked at the glass-faced shadow boxes lining the walls of her office, holding various fine laces and original versions of many of their designs.

Her gaze landed on the very first purse she'd embellished. She'd been fourteen. Had wanted a new purse for starting high school. Something cool. To give her confidence as she left Angeline behind in middle school. Duane, their stepfather, had overheard her talking to her mother about it and had gone off on an ugly rant about the purse he'd bought her for Christmas the previous year, how nothing he provided was ever good enough for her. He'd been drunk off his ass at the time, of course.

She'd taken that plain denim bag he'd bought her and, using lace made by his family's company, made herself a purse everyone loved. Including her stepfather. She'd had girls she didn't know coming up to her in the school halls, upperclassmen even, asking where she'd gotten her bag. Just like that, a business—now known as Feel Good—had started. Embellishments, a brand, distribution: all of it. They bought plain items in bulk from manufacturers and made them their own.

She'd shown up a drunk angry man and started a minor empire at fourteen. She could handle a guy who left a deposit in a cup.

"I never should have talked to Christine." Angie's face got "that" look and Amelia cringed inside. She'd promised herself she'd never, ever be the cause of that expression again. The one where Angeline feared she'd somehow compromised their relationship.

Angeline hadn't been the one to do that. Amelia had. And it was up to her to spend the rest of her life, if that was what it took, rebuilding her little sister's trust in "them."

"Of course you should have," she said, stronger now as she tended to her sister instead of to herself. "I want you completely involved in this, just like we said, and what if the call had been to tell us that there was something with the baby that needed immediate attention? A mistake on some test or something? You did the right thing, Angie. I'm just..."

"Scared?"

Yeah. "Why do you think he's calling?"

"I have no idea." Angie sat on the couch along the back wall of the smallish room, patting the

seat beside her as she reached over to a small refrigerator and pulled out an organic fruit juice
mixture. "But what I do know," she continued
once Amelia took a couple of sips, "is that he has
no legal rights to that baby. He or she is yours
and everything you signed absolutely guarantees
that."

With a head tilt to the side, Amelia studied her
sister. "You sound sure about that."

"I already called Tanya and confirmed. The second I got off the phone with Christine."

Tanya Cypress was their attorney for matters
both personal and business. Amelia had only been
in the air a couple of hours when Christine Elliott, managing director of the clinic, had called
her. While she'd been unreachable, Amelia had her
calls forwarded to Angeline. Angeline had called
Christine, and then left a voicemail for Amelia. If
Angeline had bothered to listen to her own message, she'd have known it was garbled. She hadn't.
She'd already beaten herself up over that one, apol-
ogizing several times, and Amelia hated that her
sister was still so insecure where she was concerned.

Hated herself for it. Growing up with a stepfather who was mean when he drank, and a mother
who placated him because she loved him and

couldn't bring herself to leave him, a mother who'd believed his promises that he'd stop drinking, had taken a toll on both girls. It had made them closer than many siblings, to be sure. More dependent on each other.

Which was why when, for a short time, Amelia had fallen under the control of a man she'd loved and ditched her sister at his behest, Angeline had suffered so deeply.

Her sister loved her. But Angie no longer completely trusted Amelia to have her back. Not completely.

And so she was always trying to prove to Amelia that she was good enough to deserve her loyalty. When it clearly should have been the other way around. Angie didn't need to try harder. To go above and beyond.

Amelia did.

"You have to call him, Mel."

She nodded, a surge of panic striking again as the moment bore down on her.

The father of your child.

"It's just odd that he introduced himself as 'father' rather than 'sperm donor.'"

"Just remember, he has no rights to that child. None. It's up to you to stay strong and establish that," Angie said, glancing toward Amelia's belly.

Stay strong, rather than giving in to the male influence.

She nodded again. And pulled her phone out of her pocket.

Chapter Two

Craig was riding his bike along a cliff face just outside of town that afternoon when his smart watch vibrated a call at his wrist. One glance showed him who was calling. Feet on the ground instantly, he balanced the bike between his legs and grabbed his phone out of the zipped pocket of his shorts.

He'd seen his last patient at three. Had changed clothes, mounted the bike he'd ridden to work that morning, and an hour later, he still hadn't made it home.

"Craig Harmon," he answered, exactly as he had the first time.

"What kind of doctor are you?"

No introduction. As though she assumed he'd recognize her number. Or was just rude and didn't care.

The woman wasn't impressing him as a person he could feel comfortable with raising his child.

More his problem than hers.

Still an issue, though.

"A general practitioner," he said, knowing full well that she had the upper hand.

And that he had a need that couldn't be ignored.

"Where?"

"Oceanfront Clinic." Named after the town hospital with which they were associated. If she planned to have her baby in a hospital, and in Marie Cove, it would be at Oceanfront.

But they could get to that later.

"What do you want?"

Blunt. Proving his "rude" theory correct? She sure wasn't doing anything to help him like her.

Not that she needed him to.

He was the one who needed that. To like her.

A car sped past. Moving farther off to the side, but still a safe enough distance from the cliff edge, he glanced out at the ocean that had been at his back since the day he was born. Thirty-four years of a mostly successful partnership.

What did he want?

"I'd like to meet with you," he said.

"Why?"

"I'd like to discuss that in person, if you're willing to do so."

"You have no rights to this child."

"I'm not asking for any." He frowned. In all the ways he'd played this conversation over the past few days, it hadn't gone this way. Him not being in control. Not sure of how to get to his end goals. "Per my agreement with the clinic I have the right to know who used my sperm if I ask, and I asked."

"Why are you asking?"

"A conversation," he said now. "I... For personal reasons I just need to make certain, to see for myself, that the child you're carrying is going to be well cared for. Well loved."

"Excuse me?"

"Please. That's all I'm looking for. Reassurance. And then I'm out of your life for good." Assuming he got the reassurance he was looking for.

And if he didn't? It wasn't like he had any rights to do anything about it.

So why not just let it go? Let *her* go?

"You signed the papers, giving me the right to contact the recipient of my biological donation, either to impart newly determined information regarding anything that could affect the fetus, or to request information." He suddenly saw the way ahead, right or wrong, for the sake of his unborn child. She clearly was resistant to his presence in her life. "I also have the right to request contact with the child."

"I have the right to refuse."

"What I'm telling you is that if you'll agree to meet with me, answer some basic questions, just talk, really, then I won't ever ask for any kind of contact with the child. I'll be gone. Unless, at any time, for any reason, you or the baby would contact me." Because he'd agreed to that, too.

And because he now knew that if his offspring ever needed him, for anything, he would be there.

"You'll agree to disappear after I meet with you."

"Yes." Assuming he could live with what he saw. And if not…he'd have to check with his attorney. Maybe all he could do was express his concerns to child services. To have them watch out for the baby. Maybe he couldn't even do that. He was getting way ahead of himself.

Probably for nothing. Just because he'd seen one child hurt didn't mean that he would see another.

And rudeness didn't automatically proclaim bad parenting.

"How many times?" she asked.

And he grinned. She was on her toes now—and so was he.

"Once," he said. "Preferably in your home so we can have a private conversation. I'd also like to see where the child will be raised, but if that's too weird for you, I'd settle for anyplace you choose, and pictures of the living space or anything else you'll agree to share."

"You're too weird for me."

He didn't doubt that. And didn't explain, either. Not until she'd given him what he needed.

"I need to speak with you."

"Is there a medical problem? The clinic would have said so. Unless you withheld that information from them."

"There's no medical problem. It's personal. I just need to know that my offspring is going to be well cared for."

"Why'd you agree to give up your sperm if this was going to be a problem?"

She didn't specify what she meant by "this," but he figured he knew what she meant. The her-having-his-child part.

"It's a long story. And one I'll share during our one and only meeting," he said to reassure her. He went on to give her references, even knowing that Christine had already vetted and vouched for him.

"One meeting."

"Yes."

"Do you have my address?"

"Of course not." He didn't know if she lived in Marie Cove, or had just traveled there for insemination. The Parent Portal's reputation, and uniqueness in the weight it gave to the human elements involved in sharing biological material, brought in prospective parents from all over the state and beyond.

He was willing to travel. However far it took.

"Give me some time and I'll get back to you."

She didn't say how much time. He didn't ask.

A guy with no power had to take what he could get.

Amelia got through a couple of pressing things at her desk. She had to follow up on her meetings with a particular lace designer in the south of France, and there were emails that needed her personal response. She went home and showered. And carried the voice of the doctor she hadn't met, carried his words, every step of the way. Who donated sperm and then got worried about the welfare of the child?

How bad could he be, caring about the welfare of his child?

How could she resent a man for that?

The idea that he could have any ownership of her baby petrified her. Even the thought of any intrusion into her life scared her.

And yet…there was something sweet and comforting about her baby's biological component caring about its welfare.

When all of her chores were done, she fell into bed. And slept until the following morning.

The following day, Friday, she had a full schedule and was focused and on target. In control. She thought about Craig Harmon on and off throughout the day, but couldn't seem to do so without feeling threatened, somehow. She didn't fear for her safety. Or her baby's, either. She just didn't want the man in their world and wasn't sure how much he had a right to know. How "in" he had a right to be. On her lunch break she called the Parent Portal and was put right through to Christine Elliott.

By all accounts, Craig Harmon was still a great guy. She already knew his basic family medical history. Knew that he'd graduated at the top of his undergraduate class. Knew that he was six foot one and had weighed 175 pounds at the time of his donation. She'd pored over the very thorough donor specifics provided by the Parent Portal for more than a week before she'd made her choice for her baby's biological component. That day, she learned that he'd also graduated medical school at the top of his class. And that though he'd only lived in Marie Cove for eight years, he'd been one of the Parent Portal's very first donors, introduced to Christine by the son of a local obstetrician who now worked for the Parent Portal full-time. Dr. Cheryl Miller. And she learned that Cheryl's son was a pediatrician partner in the Oceanfront Clinic—in partnership with Craig Harmon.

Clearly not a wacko out to hurt her or steal her baby.

But not anyone she wanted to meet, either. She kept reminding herself that he'd said he wanted no part in the baby's life. That he knew he had no right to that. He just wanted to reassure himself regarding the child's welfare.

Marie Cove was a small town. And she'd known that there was a possibility that her baby's biological father lived there. But there was just as good a chance that he did not. Christine attracted donors from afar, just as she did prospective parents.

She'd kind of liked the idea that the donor could be close by. In case of medical emergency or any other need she might have. She'd just never considered that the guy would look her up.

Who did that? Gave away sperm and then followed up on the recipient. Why was he doing this? Impinging on what was turning out to be the most incredible thing she'd ever done. Butting into something intimate and special. How dare he?

It seemed creepy to her. And she told Christine so.

Christine's only response had been to suggest that she speak further with Craig Harmon, just long enough to hear him out.

Clearly there were things the director couldn't tell her.

But the man would.

Things that could ultimately have an effect on her child?

For that reason alone, she picked up her phone as she waited in a designated parking spot for her grocery order to be delivered to her car.

Shopping for food that only she'd eat was kind of a lonely thing. At least now she didn't have to walk the aisles alone noticing not the tons of other single women like her who were there, but rather, the couples or mothers with kids that seemed to take up all the aisle real estate anytime she turned a corner with her cart.

Craig picked up immediately when she called. If he hadn't known her number before—and she figured that was a far-off *if*—then he surely did now. Having graduated top of his class, and all.

"I'm not saying yes or no to an in-person meet at this time," she started. "What I have decided is that I need to do this on the phone first."

"Okay."

If he was disappointed, he hid the response well. But then, he had to be the guy who walked into a room with diagnoses that were sometimes difficult to hear. He'd have expert control of his responses.

"We can talk now, or later. Your call."

"I've got one more patient to see and then have to pick up Talley. Can you call me back tonight?"

"Talley?" Did he have a child, then? One of which he already had custody?

"My dog. She's been at the hospital overnight for fluids after a severe bout of pancreatitis. I need to get her before the vet closes for the day."

His dog. She wanted to know what kind. Big? A hunter he kept for her usefulness? Or a pet? Was he an animal lover? Did it run in the family?

Nice that he was willing to pay for what had to be expensive care. Duane had once insisted that the dog Angie and Amelia had had since they were toddlers should be put to sleep, rather than receive expensive medical treatment. It turned out what they'd thought was cancer was actually a clogged tear duct, and there'd been no choice to make. But Amelia remembered the night she'd spent crying, with the dog in her arms, while she'd waited to hear.

Her groceries would be arriving any second and he had a patient to see. But Craig was still apparently waiting and hadn't said anything more.

"You've obviously got my number there, on your caller ID. Why don't you give me a call tonight when you get home and settled?"

And if he had a date...wait...no one had said...

"Are you married?" she blurted as new horrors presented themselves to her. Was he unable to have children with his wife infertile? Was that what this was about? They wanted her to...

Christine would have told her something like that.

Man...she was out of line emotionally where this baby was concerned. *And hormonal*, she admitted silently to herself.

"No. And thank you. I'll call you tonight."

Before she could respond he was gone. Leaving her to fret about the fact that he wasn't out of her life yet.

Chapter Three

He'd driven his SUV to work that morning, in deference to needing to pick up Talley, and skipped his usual bike ride when he got home that evening. His girl, a twelve-year-old collie, was better, but still not herself and he wasn't eager to leave her. She was older, but hadn't quite reached the life expectancy for her breed. Still, he knew that within the next couple of years her time with him would come to a close.

Just as Tricia's life had done. Come to a close. Talley had been her dog...

His phone rang just as he was getting Talley settled on a fleece blanket on the couch. Still in the brown pants and beige shirt and tie he'd worn to work, he flopped down next to her, settling into the corner, wishing he'd grabbed a beer out of the refrigerator first.

He'd read a recent study that said two beers a night was a good heart-health regimen. Any more than that and the results went backward.

"Thank you for calling," he said as soon as he pushed to accept the call. Ready to get his answers and move on. The woman could be married. Or engaged. Or with a significant other.

She was the last of the three recipients of his specimen—which had been destroyed at his request after he'd seen firsthand what people could do to their kids. This one remaining detail was all he had to handle.

"I give you my word, I'm not out to cause you stress, nor do I have any intention of making your life uncomfortable in any way."

"What do you want to know?"

That his child would be raised in a loving, happy, secure home.

And how did he quantify that?

He had to know that his child would never hurt or want for anything.

No one could guarantee a pain-free existence. There probably wasn't such a thing. Life wasn't meant to be without challenges. He just wished to God he'd been more aware of the possibilities before he'd donated to science as a favor to a friend.

"The truth is, I'm not sure. I was hoping that a conversation with you, meeting you, would show me what I needed to see, and that would be it."

Talley lifted her head. Laid it on his thigh and closed her eyes. He petted her head. Slowly. Lingering with his palm on her neck, and then back again. Just a light touch, enough for her to know he was there, and for him to reassure himself that she was.

"I really need to know what's going on here or I'm going to have to ask you to not contact me again," she said.

"I need to know that the children that I helped create are in happy, healthy environments."

"Children? You're calling other women, as well?"

"There were three. You're the last."

"You've contacted the other two? Met with them?"

"One was an unsuccessful attempt. A pregnancy did not result."

"And the other?"

"Resulted in a ten-year-old girl who is a delight."

"You've met her?"

"No." And he didn't need to do so. "Her parents couldn't conceive. Their genetics weren't compatible. But her father...there's not a man who dotes more on his little girl."

"You met the parents, then? Just not the child?"

"Just him. The father." Kent Sanders.

"Are they here in Marie Cove?"

"Nope. They're in Oregon. He's a contractor. I saw a photo of her on his lap riding around on his backhoe and laughing up at him."

There'd been more. A lot more. All delivered to him through Kent. The family had been happy to share their lives with him. They'd been so incredibly thankful. He'd seen school reports. Family photos. They'd even opened up her medical records to him—their offer, not his request—because he was a doctor. And because they wanted to give him the peace of mind he sought, since he'd given so much more to them.

The rest wasn't his to share. But he needed Amelia Grace to know that he truly wasn't after her child, any more than he'd been after the Sanderses' girl.

"I'm looking for peace," he told her. That was it. Just a mind and heart at peace.

"And you think I can give it to you?"

"I hope to God you can."

"And if I can't? What happens then?"

He had no idea.

Amelia's sudden strong surge of desire to help him was not welcome.

The man hadn't answered her last question. What happened if she couldn't magically give Craig Harmon the peace he was looking for?

Hell, some days—most days—it felt like she was still seeking her own peace. She was beginning to think it was a mirage.

None of which she planned to share with the recipient of her phone call. She wanted to get rid of him, not send him further into need.

Pulling her phone away from her ear, she checked to see that they were still connected. If he was waiting for her to invite an invasion of her private life, as that Oregon family had, he was holding on in vain.

And yet…she wasn't hanging up, either.

Which was odd. He was no one to her. She felt no connection between him and the precious child that was growing inside her.

"Why did you donate samples?" She'd asked once before. He'd said he'd give her the long story when they met. She wasn't agreeing to meet with him. She was just talking.

"I was an only child in a close-knit family. My folks and I, we're still close. They wanted more children, but couldn't conceive a second. When I got to med school, I met Tad Miller and heard about what Christine was trying to do, starting up the Parent Portal with money left to her by her mother, making it a place where family came first, in an open environment where biologicals would give each other contact rights… Christine had couples wanting families, but she didn't have men knocking down her door to leave viable sperm. My friend, Tad, was donating, his mother was involved with the clinic, and…it just sounded like a decent thing to do."

Her heart lurched. She moved to the kitchen. Polished the chrome faucet with the bottom of her shirt. Adjusted the table in the nook, making certain that three of the four chairs were situated to catch the best of the ocean views from the bay window. She usually sat in the chair that faced the kitchen, but had been moving it around a bit. Just trying out the other spots. The views—one of the main reasons she'd purchased the two-thousand-square-foot luxury unit when they'd moved their headquarters to town the previous year—really were spectacular. Even at night.

Shortly after she'd moved in she'd spent most of one night sitting at that table with a bottle of wine, watching the lights of boats and barges, and the occasional cruise ship, bob out in the far distance. From her sixth-floor vantage point, she could also see the two blocks between her and the water.

The man had donated for altruistic purposes. Not money. At least, that's what he wanted her to believe.

"How much did she pay you?"

"Nothing. We did, however, get extra credit in our medical cell biology class," he added.

A-ha. So he'd benefitted personally.

Having graduated with honors, though…she wasn't sure how much he'd needed that extra credit. It certainly wouldn't have been enough to catapult him to the top of the class.

Dropping one thigh to the chair with the most direct ocean view, Amelia half sat in the near-dark, contemplating a cup of decaffeinated green tea. With two spoonfuls of honey. Because it was Friday night.

"So you donated, but didn't feel completely good about having done so," she surmised, in no real hurry to end the conversation.

Craig Harmon was more interesting than television. Angie was still in LA, out with some friends. They'd invited her along, but they were at a wine bar and since she was consuming zero alcohol for the foreseeable future...

Besides, they weren't her friends. Or even their mutual ones. Angie was catching up with the high school friends who'd seen her through the worst year and a half of her life. The time when Amelia had hardly seen her.

Because of choices Amelia made.

"Have you ever made a choice that you so deeply regret you can't let it go?"

She lurched, almost dropping the phone. Had she spoken aloud? She actually did a double check on her last few seconds to reassure herself that she had not opened her mouth.

"Why do you ask that?" Her tone was a little sharp. She didn't apologize.

"Because if you had, you might be a little better able to understand."

Yes, she'd made a choice, which had led to continuously bad ones. She'd hurt those she loved most, those who'd stood by her her entire life, and she wasn't sure she'd ever be able to forgive herself. Or trust herself, more like it.

No, that wasn't right, either. She'd made other

choices since, and because of them, she did trust herself. She was never, ever going to allow a man to have control over her again. Not ever.

She was her mother's daughter. That wasn't her fault. Couldn't be helped. But knowing that she, like her mother, had an inexplicable need to please the man in her life, to subjugate self and other loved ones, to sacrifice the feelings of others to fulfill his needs, to put him first no matter what…she could be accountable to that knowledge and keep herself from hurting her loved ones by staying away from any form of long-term commitment to a man.

"I'm listening," was all she said, forgoing the idea of tea for the moment. She hadn't really even had dinner yet. The couple of blended fruit pouches she'd consumed on the drive home didn't count. She'd been dreading the conversation with Dr. Harmon. Hadn't had much of an appetite.

Which seemed a bit extreme to her at the moment.

In the dark, safe in her home with the ocean in front of her, a simple phone conversation couldn't hurt anything.

Chapter Four

He was a doctor. Healing people was his business. When had Craig himself become the one in need of healing? How had he let himself get to this point?

Shaking his head, Craig sat with Talley, not allowing himself to take comfort from her presence anymore, but rather, watching over her as he spoke to Amelia.

"I was in a six-year relationship," he said, sifting through facts to make Amelia Grace understand.

He didn't need her sympathy. Silence hung on the line.

"The woman had a child. A son, Gavin, who was two when I came into the picture. The boy's father never had anything to do with him. Tricia was just as happy to have him out of her life and never went after him for child support."

"Define 'six-year relationship.' Were you married? Living together? Just seeing each other?"

The question was fair. Until she'd asked it, he hadn't been sure she was still interested in hearing what he had to say.

"Living together," he told her. "I wanted to get married. Asked her several times." That might make him look like there was something wrong with him, not marriage material. But her opinion of him wasn't at stake here. His peace of mind, while causing her little to no stress, was the immediate goal.

To ensure the end goal.

A healthy and happy child.

"Did she have something against marriage in general? Or just marriage to you?"

He relaxed a bit more into the couch. The woman on the other end of the line…her forthrightness was kind of refreshing.

"Marriage in general," he was kind of glad to report, though the fact made no difference to their outcome. He didn't need Amelia to like him— didn't plan to be in her life long enough.

"Tricia used to say that nothing lasted forever.

And she didn't want us to be together because we were tied, legally or financially. She wanted us to be together just because we both still wanted to be," he found himself explaining further. On the surface he'd understood Tricia's explanation, which had been logical enough to keep him around. But he'd never agreed with her.

He wanted a wife. An equal partner in all aspects of life. Legal. Financial. And emotional. He believed in family forever. If that made him some kind of sap, then so be it.

He wanted what his parents still had after forty years together.

Life was unpredictable. He saw that every day at the clinic. Seemingly healthy young people developing life-threatening problems. Elderly patients ready to go who continued to live and grow older.

Family and love: those seemed to him to be the glue that kept happiness present. Both certainly played a huge part in the healing process. He'd seen evidence of that time and time again.

None of which was pertinent here.

And Tricia—maybe she'd somehow known, on some level, that her life was to be short. The thought offered an odd comfort now and then. And didn't really ring true. If she'd known, she'd have made arrangements for Gavin…

"I'm assuming you broke up?" Amelia's tone seemed to have softened by the time she broke into the silence that had fallen.

"Tricia was killed in a car accident a couple of years ago," he said. "A drunk driver crossed a double yellow line just outside of town."

"This town? Marie Cove?" She sounded surprised. "You hooked up with her when you moved here?"

"Before, actually, but we made it official when I moved here." He glanced around the home he'd moved into upon graduation from medical school when he'd agreed to be a part of the start-up, physician-owned clinic at Oceanfront. "I met Tricia through Dr. Miller, Tad's mother. I don't know how much you know about Marie Cove's history, but the town has long been a haven for LA's rich and famous who want to be able to exist in a somewhat normal, if luxurious, atmosphere. Tricia grew up here, the daughter of one of the big city's wealthiest plastic surgeons and a married man she never named, but whom Tricia firmly believed her mother loved until the day she died."

More than he'd needed to say. Or maybe, exactly what she'd needed to hear to be able to ascertain what he was asking of her. Either way, the conversation wasn't unpleasant.

"So she was already gone before Tricia's accident?"

"She died before Gavin was born." She'd killed herself with a drug and alcohol cocktail, due to the pain of loving a married man. After the funeral, Tricia had slept with the first guy she'd come in contact with, got pregnant and nearly three years later met Craig. It was all neatly documented in his mind. Facts that fit together in a way that made sense to him. Facts that helped distract him from the gaping hole inside him—left not just by Tricia, but by the boy he'd loved like a son, thought of as a son, and then lost.

"Oh."

"Oh, what?"

"Oh, no."

Sitting up abruptly, Craig slowed his motions as Talley's head popped up, her eyes wide and alert as she studied him.

"What's going on?" he asked when there was nothing further from the other end of the line.

"Nothing. Just… Gavin… What happened to him? Because you'd have said you had a son to feed or something if you had him, instead of just a dog to pick up. And there were no grandparents on Tricia's side to take him with her mother gone and her father unnamed. The dad was just an after-the-funeral thing. So that leaves…he was in the car with his mother, wasn't he?"

It was a hard thing for him to get right with in his mind.

"No."

"You do have him, then?"

"No."

"It's not good, is it?"

"Tricia had money. Gavin's father knew that. He was named on Gavin's birth certificate. I knew the guy was no good. I petitioned the court, promising Gavin that I'd keep us together…"

Again with the facts…the rest of it…how did you go on when you could hardly draw air? When you felt so helpless you weren't sure you'd ever be in charge of your life, or be able to make things right ever again?

"Oh, God. I know where this is going."

Partially, she probably did.

"The jerk got custody, you lost your son because he wasn't biologically yours and now…"

"Not only that but the jerk also *abused* his son, but even when family services got involved, they refused to allow him to be adopted."

"By you."

Or anyone.

"Where is he now?"

"Living with a stepmother who doesn't give a rat's ass about him. Gavin's father got married so that he could name her guardian of his son, and the woman plays along because she likes getting money from his trust fund for his care."

"You're kidding. I mean, I know you aren't, but...what about the abuse? How does the father have custody?"

"He doesn't. She does. They live separately. He has visitation rights. They've moved out of state and, last I heard, Gavin had done a stint in juvenile detention for putting a kid in his class in the hospital." He burned, with physical acid in his gut, every time he thought about it.

Anger issues had been Gavin's diagnosis, not that anyone was doing anything more than absolutely legally necessary to help him. They did what they had to so that they could keep their hands on his money. Craig was as certain as he could be without actual confirmation that Gavin knew that, too. He was a smart kid.

One with a great heart and a load of potential.

And who was likely headed for prison if someone didn't intervene soon. Lord knew Craig had tried to visit with Gavin, to be there for him. So hard that The Jerk had finally taken out a restraining order against him, claiming that Craig was trying to interfere with his ability to parent his child.

He'd gone to court. Explained to the judge. And while the order had been denied, the judge had firmly suggested that Craig not try to contact Gavin again, explaining to Craig that it was to give the boy's father a chance to form a relationship with him. It was state mandated. And though Craig had continued to appeal, to try, he'd been shot down by the state supreme court the month before.

He could tell the judge had been on his side. But the law had not been.

"Last you heard...so you still have some contact?"

"Only if he contacts me. And then I have to let his father know."

"Has he contacted you?"

"No."

"But you keep a watch over him."

"I hired someone to keep track of him as much as is permitted. And if I ever find a legal way to help him, I will do so."

"You said his mother died two years ago."

"Yes."

"Are you still living in the house you two shared?"

"Yes."

"The house where Gavin lived?"

"Yes." But if she thought he was living off of Tricia's money, as well...

"I bought the house from her the first time I asked her to marry me and she declined. I agreed to stay with her on the condition that I owned the home." He'd figured that way Gavin would always have his childhood home to come to, whether Craig and Tricia stayed together or not, and had told her so.

Tricia had cried at the thought of it. And had still charged him market value for the home. Which he'd willingly paid. He'd never cared about her money. He cared about her.

And Gavin.

About their family.

Talley looked over at him and for a second there Craig allowed himself to believe that the dog knew what he'd been thinking. And was thanking him for keeping what was left of that family—her and him—together.

"This is why you regret your choice to make it possible for your children to be in the world without you having any way to keep them safe."

He wouldn't have put it quite like that, but admitted, "Yes."

And then he added, "I am now grossly aware that not everyone is meant to be a parent. And that children are completely dependent on those raising them to help them reach their potential. I know, firsthand, that some parents can hurt their children and that the courts can't always save them. Or can only do so for certain periods of time at which point the parents get a second chance. And sometimes a third and fourth, depending on the circumstances. And the age of the child." He could go on. And on. But he stopped himself.

"If you'd like to make an appointment to stop by my home sometime this weekend, I will let you inside for a short time."

He had to replay her words in his head before her offer hit home.

"And only with the very firm understanding that no matter what you think, this child is mine. Not yours."

Okay. Hell's bells. He was being given the road to recovery. To at least some level of emotional freedom from regret. "I understand."

"You have no say, no ownership, no rights to make even one single suggestion where my baby is concerned."

"I understand." But she didn't seem to. He didn't want her baby. He just wanted her to be a decent parent. And finally felt free to start probing her background.

"I didn't ask Christine, but are you married?"

Which mattered only because her husband should then have a say about when he visited their home.

"No."

No reason to feel any hint of relief there. To the contrary, he'd rather his child have a two-parent home. As he had. So when one adult was ill or otherwise distracted by life's responsibilities, there was another to step up. Children's needs didn't wait around for convenient moments.

"You live alone?"

"Yes."

"Is there a significant other in your life?"

"No." Her tone sharpened.

And he knew when to quit.

Agreeing to meet her at home the following afternoon at four, he rang off. And thought maybe he should turn off his phone just in case she tried to contact him to cancel.

He didn't do it. He wasn't out of his head. But the thought had been there. So he entertained it. Which was why it took him another couple of seconds to realize he was smiling—and looking forward to the next afternoon.

Only for peace of mind's sake. Or so he told himself. He was going to meet the woman carrying his biological child. He couldn't really wrap his mind around that one—but there was good feeling in it.

Tossing his phone on the cushion on the other side of his dog, he jumped up, ready to find something for dinner. He wondered if there was some small gift he could take the next day when he officially met the mother of his child.

As he left the room, he glanced back at the dog, to see if she was awake and might take some food. Talley was glaring at him. Like he'd even need to wonder whether or not he should pick something up. Of course he should. The woman was carrying his baby.

Chapter Five

Amelia worked Saturday, catching up on everything that had fallen behind during her four days in the south of France. The laces Feel Good bought from Duane's family business were fine for jeans and purses—and quite lovely on the pillowcases and towels they'd branched into a few years before. With the possibility of precious-metal jewelry embellishments lingering on the horizon, she'd needed some finer but affordable lace, at a price point that would allow them to sell the finished product and make a profit. They were starting out small with lace embellished jewelry—just one design in time for summer weddings.

Until she'd had the call from Craig Harmon, ideas had been flowing faster than she could get them sketched.

It wasn't like she'd had time recently to sit with her sketch pad. Being the boss sometimes took precedence over being a designer, along with Angie. The lace embellished jewelry idea had been hers. She had a wholesaler from China offering the basic jewelry pieces—mostly various wires and simple circular pendants that they'd embellish.

They did most of their design and desk work, marketing, etc., out of the new headquarters in Marie Cove, and had a small factory and forty employees in east LA, where the actual inventory was made put together. Payroll and accounting were outsourced, as was a lot of the public relations and advertising help, but she wanted to pursue the idea of moving everything in-house—growing from the inside out. Angie hadn't fully jumped on board with that idea.

But she hadn't said no. Amelia wasn't ready to push her sister for fear of any rift it might cause between them. She needed Angie to feel validated, welcome. Wanted.

As her mind started to wander toward the much more personal business on her agenda later that afternoon, Amelia consciously refused and focused on Feel Good. When was growth healthy and when was it too much? She didn't want to ignore Angie's more financially conservative perspective, but Amelia was the one with the business degree. Angie's degree was in marketing and she handled a lot of the in-person meetings with accounts. They'd both minored in art design. With their success, they showed every sign of being able to sell stock options someday. It made good business sense to allow the business to breathe itself into whatever it could be.

Angie wanted to keep boundaries around Feel Good. To keep it small and in the family.

So, for now, Amelia was focusing only on growing the family, instead of the company. Giving in to Angie because her relationship with her sister was more important than extended business growth.

Which brought her back around to Craig Harmon, anyway. He seemed like a decent guy. One who meant well. Who was asking for something valid—if way too abstract for her—and going about it in the proper way as defined by the contracts they'd signed.

Just because she'd never imagined this particular scenario when she'd considered the stipulations to which she'd agreed didn't mean his contact was in any way wrong. Or even inappropriate. She'd talked to Tanya, too. She wasn't legally obligated to meet with him. But he had the right to ask.

He could check to see that the baby she had was well, and recheck within reasonable time frames. He also had the right to request contact with the child. She didn't have to grant that, either. She just couldn't stop him from asking, unless he harassed her.

Bottom line was, she could, at any time, tell Craig Harmon to leave her alone. And he had a right to certain generic information regarding the well-being of the baby she carried.

It was all in there.

And knowing it all, even with Craig Harmon's recent communication, she would have still chosen the Parent Portal and signed the contracts. While she had mixed emotions about the male biological component of her child, she was kind of curious to meet him. He couldn't have her child, but her heart definitely went out to him regarding his situation with his son. And her respect for him had grown hugely, too. He didn't give up when it came to doing what was right. Fighting for those he cared about.

Something she'd failed to do with Angie. And her top priority these days. She was going to do whatever it took to care for her small family. She'd already made arrangements to bank cord blood. And had purchased all of the necessary items to baby-proof her home. Angie had hired someone to install the cupboard and door latches in both their homes.

Amelia dialed her sister as she drove into her private garage Saturday afternoon, half an hour before she was due to see Craig.

Angie was having lunch at home with their mom in Santa Barbara while Duane played golf. She'd had a meeting with a lucrative boutique to be the exclusive carrier of Feel Good apparel there.

"Hey, when's that guy coming to install the baby-safety items?" she asked as soon as her sister picked up. If Angie was telling Mom about Craig Harmon, she didn't want to know. She hadn't asked her sister not to say anything, but hoped she wouldn't. Their mom had a tendency to worry and both Angie and Amelia fed off her emotions.

At least, that was the theory. One of many that had come via the counseling she'd sought after breaking up with Mike.

"The first Saturday in February," Angie said. So two weeks away. "I just left Mom's. Lunch was good," she continued. "And no bottles. I checked all the usual places and anywhere else I could think of."

Amelia had done her share of checking, as well. Not in a while, though. Duane had been sober for several years. Since that last horrible time when he'd gone after Angie...

Her little sister had called her that awful day, but she'd blown her off. Figuring Angie's tears were just more of the drama from which she'd chosen to escape. Mike's rhetoric. The whole "her choosing to escape the drama of her family life" thing. It had sounded good to her at the time. But putting thoughts like that in her head, asking things like that of her, had really just been one of the many ways in which he'd isolated her from everyone else in her life she'd ever loved.

So he could have it all. Have all of her. Thankfully she'd wised up before he'd consumed her completely.

"How was Mom?" Amelia asked, heading toward the back, secure entrance of her building.

Angie talked about their mother's charity work. Mentioned one of her friends who'd just become a grandmother. And finished with, "She mentioned you half a dozen times, Mel. You really need to drive up here and see her."

Angie was right, of course. But Amelia hated

the tone in her sister's voice. The one that reminded Amelia that her little sister still believed
that Amelia was their mother's favorite child. That
she needed to see Amelia more than she needed
to see Angie.

She wanted to believe that belief was just more
of Angie's insecurity. But knew it wasn't. Margaret
Grace did appear to prefer being around Amelia.
Amelia's practicality made their mother feel secure where Angie's constant nurturing made her
feel old. At least, that was the theory.

Another takeaway from counseling.

"Did you tell her about Craig Harmon?"

"No. Why would I? He's a phone call. A blip.
Why make him a bigger part of our lives?"

Having spoken with her mom and Duane before
having herself inseminated, Amelia knew that,
while they wished she were married, they were
fully supportive of her choice. Had offered to do
anything they could to help her and had already
bought a portable crib and high chair for when the
baby came to visit. Since Duane quit drinking,
things had definitely improved. And...you made
do. She loved her mom and the only way to have
her in her life was to accept Duane and try to focus
on what was good about him...

"Because they'd like to know that the donor is

a doctor," she said now. And then added, "But I'm glad you didn't. I'd just as soon keep this between me and you."

People were curious. She generally disliked questions of a personal nature—since Mike. Her life didn't hold up as well under scrutiny as she'd like and those who knew about that had reason to doubt the wisdom of her choices. Since she struggled with enough pressure in that area from herself, she preferred not to open herself up to more of it.

"Me, too," Angie said. "You talked to him. It's done."

With a huge, uncomfortable twinge of unease, she stood in the lobby, keeping her back to the security guard over in the corner, and told Angie that she was getting on the elevator and was about to lose her.

The complete truth.

And an "out," too. She hadn't told Angie about the upcoming meeting. Only that she'd spoken to the doctor the night before. She'd called Angie right after she'd hung up from Craig last night.

And hadn't wanted to worry her.

Or, another theory that held possibility, she hadn't wanted Angie to doubt her. To think that she'd fall for the doctor and cut Angie out.

Mostly, she just wanted to get the upcoming meet done so that Craig Harmon truly was out of their lives and she was free to be the single mom she wanted and needed to be, raising a happy, healthy, well-adjusted child with tons of familial support. But there could be some truth to the not wanting Angie to doubt her, too.

Craig had the perfect little gift for Amelia Grace. Unfortunately, he'd also been on call at the clinic that morning and had been running so late that he'd only been able to "wrap" his gift by shoving it in an empty X-ray envelope and wrapping the little string around the button closure. Still in his navy pants, light blue long-sleeved shirt and blue striped tie, he smoothed hair back behind his ear with a nervous hand as he waited to be cleared through security and gain access to the elevator that would take him up to Amelia's condo.

He'd been in the plush establishment before, a few times. The chief of staff at Oceanfront Hospital lived in the penthouse.

And he couldn't imagine himself as a kid—or any child—living there. Where would he run? Or jump on beds? Where would he holler along with the video game? Or learn to throw baseballs?

A nearby park was the obvious answer for that one.

Still, a kid shouldn't have to always be circumspect at home. He wasn't privy to the owner's actual rules and regulations in the Oceanview Towers, but it was pretty clear that everyone in the place was expected to act with some measure of decorum. Out of respect for their neighbors.

All of whom were clearly wealthy and could afford to be assured their lives wouldn't be interrupted by neighborly irritations.

Amelia opened her door just as he got off the elevator. She wore a pair of dark blue jeans with white lace butterflies adorning one leg from shapely thigh to deliciously thin ankle, a black T-shirt with a white and blue lace strip around a pocket that molded a far too enticingly shaped breast and black wedged sandals.

"Each floor in each building houses two units," she told him as he glanced down both sides of the smallish hallway before entering her place. "And there are separate elevators that stop at each floor, for each of the two units."

So not quite a private elevator, but a private entrance for each floor.

Which meant a private hallway. Nice.

The space wasn't big enough for a kid to run. Or throw a ball. He could probably get away with a holler or two, though.

He tried to make the thought occupy his mind.

Instead, he caught a glimpse of the sexy shape of her butt in front of him, leading him into Amelia Grace's private space.

Dry mouth wasn't usual for him. Nor was reticence when it came to entering a beautiful woman's apartment.

"You having second thoughts?" she asked, turning, when he didn't immediately follow her in. "Or you've seen enough to allay your fears and we're done here?"

He'd been expecting a visibly pregnant woman— though he knew she wouldn't be showing yet. He knew every change her body would make, and approximately when, throughout the birthing process. Still, he'd had this maternal vision in his head. Someone who reminded him of his mother, maybe.

Not an incredibly poised, beautiful woman who had his body needing this to be a social call.

She reached for the door handle. Afraid she was going to close it on him, he stepped forward. Shoved the envelope out toward her.

"You brought me an X-ray?" she asked, frowning. "I'm Amelia, by the way."

He nodded. "I'm Craig."

Dr. Craig Harmon. An intelligent, respectable man. Not this moron who seemed to be taking over his life for the moment.

"I know." She gave a peremptory nod. "Security cleared you through…" The last ended on a bit of an uptilt in her voice, like she was asking a question.

Or asking if he was in his right mind and remembered what he was doing there.

A fair question. Not that he wanted her to know that.

She'd yet to really look at him. Could he hope she hadn't noticed he was acting imbecilic?

He stepped inside, followed her through a large, marble foyer, past an archway leading to a formal living room, by a door with a couch and love seat arrangement with a large-screen television and through a door on the other side that held a desk, a couple of wingback chairs with colorful floral fabric and two walls lined with bookcases.

"Have a seat," she said, indicating one of the floral chairs, while she took the other and put his gift offering down on the small round table between them.

"It's not an X-ray," he said, nodding toward the envelope. "It's a family photo, my parents and I, taken when I graduated from medical school, along with baby pictures of the three of us. And also the results of the DNA testing we did last year. I'm mostly Scottish on my father's side, and Irish on my mother's."

Whether that meant anything to her at all, he had no idea. He was winging it here. And feeling the crunch as, for one of the first times he could remember, he felt like he was failing.

"The pictures…a lot of times when a baby is born…you always hear the parents and grandparents saying who the baby looks like. I just thought you might want to know—if your child is born with a thick head of hair and all of the babies in your family have been born bald, you'd have some frame of reference. You know, rather than just wondering about unknown components in your child's heritage."

It was why the Parent Portal was so immediately popular. Because it offered alternative parenting opportunities with more comprehensive family information, and an ability to reach out to the donor if necessary or desired. So many clinics just dealt with legalities and basic health information required by law—forgetting about the human element that went into creating a baby. The Parent Portal took into consideration that the child itself might someday want to meet the donor whose genes he or she carried.

Amelia didn't pick up the envelope. She pursed

her bottom lip. Giving him an inescapable urge to kiss it.

He hadn't spent that much time without being with a woman. Had never had a problem attracting lovely, willing partners.

Putting his completely out of character libido down to the fact that he'd never before met a woman who was carrying his child, he looked around him. Tried again to imagine a child growing up in Amelia's atmosphere.

While the chairs were a little feminine for his taste, he liked the sense of happiness they seemed to give to the room.

Nothing was out of place, though. Nor had it been in the other two rooms he'd glimpsed. Or the hall, with its ornate mirror and expensive-looking side table with a lap and assorted garnishments—mostly with splashes of color.

Had she cleaned on his behalf?

Did she realize a baby, and all the resulting paraphernalia that seemed to trail into every room, was going to completely disrupt her perfection here? Would she be able to handle that?

Would she welcome it?

"Three of the four of us who hung together through medical school have kids," he said. "Or, in my case, had," he said. He'd been about to tell her how homes were transformed with colorful plastic gadgets that all made sounds and had blinking lights taking up space along walls and in the middle of floors. About the miniature motorized four-wheelers for three-year-olds.

And foam floor mats with letters and numbers splashed all over them.

Her expression tensed, almost as though she'd read his mind.

"If you had a choice, would you want the baby I'm carrying?" Accusation seemed to lace through every word.

"Absolutely not! If I had a choice, you wouldn't be carrying a baby at all." He heard himself, shuddered inwardly, and added, "You wouldn't be carrying a child with my genes."

Chin jutting out, bringing his attention to them again, she looked him in the eye for the first time.

He could swear she'd just shot him full of testosterone.

Sitting there trying to hide the evidence, wishing he hadn't yet passed over the envelope, wondering what she'd think if he grabbed it back up, Craig tried to find something unattractive about her.

And only got more turned on when he couldn't find anything.

This meeting wasn't going at all like it was supposed to. He didn't even generally go for redheads. Not that her hair was red. More like brown with tinges of sunset in it.

He needed the distractions of a football field, with big guys coming at him. Or at least so he could put that much distance between him and a woman he was having a hard time remembering he'd just met.

A woman who, by her expression, and the lack of ebullience in her voice during their previous conversation, had made it pretty clear she wanted nothing to do with him.

It was time for him to find his peace of mind and get the hell out of there.

Chapter Six

Wow. Her baby had a great chance of being gorgeous.

It was the first time Amelia had actually thought about how the child she was carrying might look. She'd cared about biology. About genetics and health. About creating an emotional environment that would promote happiness. About love and support.

Maybe she'd kind of assumed he or she would have hazel eyes and auburn or red hair, because she and Angie and Mom all had them. Angie's hair being a deep red, while hers and their mother's was more brown with natural reddish highlights.

Craig Harmon had blond hair, a bit long, and she kind of liked it that way, with a little wayward piece behind his ear curling slightly. His eyes, when she finally met his gaze, were as blue as the ocean on a perfect day. No doubt blue. Pure. And they seemed to look right inside her.

She couldn't have that.

"I just can't help feeling that you have an ulterior motive here," she told him, more because she felt the need to push him away than because she was ready to have this conversation. "You say you want no part of my child's life, and yet, here you are."

"I am halfway responsible for the life you are creating. That child is my biological responsibility."

He wasn't making her feel any better.

"I completely understand…and sympathize with…the tragedy you've been through. Losing not only your life partner, but the child you'd raised as a son…and then finding yourself powerless when you knew he was being mistreated… I get it. I really do. I just…it occurs to me that you could be trying to fill some of the holes left in your life. You lost your son because he wasn't biologically yours, so now you're trying connect with the child that *is* a result of your biological component."

No more than that. A test-tube contribution. Science.

He bent his head, elbows on his spread knees, hands clasped.

His fingers were long, on hands that looked like they could take on the world, or a tiny hand, with equal success.

She wondered what those long legs would look like in jeans? And that torso, without an extra pound anywhere…shirtless.

She shook her head. So it was kind of pleasant to know that her offspring had a handsome father— his state of dress was nothing to her.

Nothing.

His head raised abruptly, before she could pull her gaze away. Those blue eyes caught her staring.

"All I want is freedom," he told her. "The situation with Gavin…it just hit home…that not all kids are born to good parents. There's so much out of my control."

Her baby being one of them, she wanted to say. And didn't want to say, too. The man was truly struggling. And she wasn't a heartless bitch, even though she tried to pretend to be sometimes. Being prickly kept people away. The fewer people she let get close, the less chance she had of screwing up again. Of becoming all in and letting her actions be controlled by her feelings for another. Making choices that maybe weren't the best ones just to keep someone else happy.

She couldn't make Craig Harmon happy. He wasn't her responsibility. Her life.

"I just couldn't stop thinking how irresponsible I was to just give someone, anyone, the ability to have my child. That I could have been party to a child living with needless pain, while I'm out here living the good life. It wasn't my goal, or intention, at all, when I donated. I just didn't think... Like I said before, haven't you ever done anything that you so deeply regret you can't let it go? I'm just trying to make it right. Again, I'm here for freedom."

Oh, God. She felt those words clear to her soul. All the way inside, as deep as it got. Hell, yes, she'd done something that she regretted so deeply she couldn't let it go. She'd let a man she'd thought she'd loved convince her to turn her back on her sister. Her friends. She'd ditched them all because Mike had told her she had to think of him, put him first, because of the "family" they were going to be, to create, for the rest of their lives.

She'd listened so exclusively to him she'd been deaf when Angie had called, devastated and needing her, the day Duane had burst into her room and told her she was a cancer in all their lives. She knew Duane said horrible things when he was drunk. Angie knew it, too. They'd both lived through them more times than she could count.

She hadn't known that that day was different. That Angie had been home alone with Duane. That even when he'd seen her standing there in pajama bottoms and a bra, in the process of changing, he hadn't turned his back or left her room. He'd stood there humiliating her with verbal abuse...

Standing, she went to the pretty cherrywood desk across and down from them, grabbed the folder, which was the only nondecorative item on top. No computer screen in the library, though her laptop was on the keyboard shelf just beneath the desktop.

"Here," she said, handing him the folder she'd only just then decided for sure to give to him. She'd been debating. Had had it ready...

"That's everything I could think of to show you that you have no need to worry. You can see by my home that I'm financially secure. Or—" she cocked her head "—I suppose I could be living above my means, in over my head, but you can look us up. My sister and I own Feel Good, a company and brand of apparel and household items for women. We're privately owned, but we still file profit and loss statements."

He didn't open the folder. Seemed more interested in her taking her seat next to him again. The look in his eye—kind…and appreciative?—made her want to smile. She nodded toward the folder instead.

"In there you'll find how conscientious and aware I am. How willing I am to do everything possible to provide for every chance of well-being for my baby. I've opted to have every test I can have at this point—all the screenings and blood work, even those that were optional. I'm sure you're far more familiar with them than I am, but all of the results are there, along with my medical records, which will show you that I live a healthy lifestyle. You also see the paperwork in there showing that I've already arranged to bank the cord blood, which isn't inexpensive, and I hope that will help assure you that I am educating myself and taking all available options in the event that my baby is faced with medical challenges. I've got a man coming two weeks from today to install all of the baby-safe latches on my drawers and cupboards, and a security camera for the nursery that will show on a monitor in my room."

She planned to have the baby in a portable crib in her room for the first few months, as recommended to her at the new parenting class she'd taken.

"You can take as long as you like to look over everything," she told him. "I'm going for some juice—would you like anything? Tea? Coffee? I can do a cup at a time."

"What kind of juice?" He seemed to be absorbed by the folder.

And she kind of felt like she'd pulled her pants down or something. Not totally in a bad way.

"I have several," she said, not sure she was talking just about juice at that point. She had several thoughts about him. Several desires, too, all of a sudden, which were totally inappropriate and not what she was going to offer him. "Cranberry-orange, pineapple-coconut, strawberry-banana…"

He'd looked up at her, his expression seeming… impressed?

"What?"

"Strawberry-banana is a staple for me," he said. "I stock up when it's on sale…"

"Two glasses of strawberry-banana coming up," she told him, turning quickly and getting her ass out of there.

* * *

Her medical records pulled his head out of his ass and back into what was a critically important moment in his life. He'd been given the chance to see to the well-being of a future child that carried his genes. He let his brain take over completely as he studied test results and several years' worth of physical exams and statistics, as well.

Her blood pressure tended to run a little lower than average but in a completely healthy way. Her blood work was stellar. Heart rate perfect. Body weight to height above average—also in a good way. She'd only gained two pounds in the fourteen and a half weeks she'd been pregnant. Also within normal range.

The cord blood bank she'd chosen was one with which he was familiar. A patient he'd seen the previous year and then had to refer due to a leukemia diagnosis, a year-old boy, was now testing cancer free, due, in large part, to treatment with his own cord blood, and it had been stored at the same bank. He'd just seen the boy's father for his annual physical the week before and had seen a video from the father's phone of a healthy, happy two-year-old riding a motorized train around the kitchen.

Amelia walked in the room just as he was finishing up. Handing her the folder, in exchange for a tall glass of juice, he took a long sip. She dropped the folder back on the desk and he waited for her to join him.

Hoping she didn't think that they were done.

While everything she'd shown him had eased his mind, considerably, a lot more went into parenting than physical health.

Some of the most critical aspects of a child's well-being came from environmental and emotional stability.

When she sipped from her glass, but didn't immediately sit back down, he glanced toward the folder on her desk. "You had the NIPT," he said, naming a noninvasive blood test she'd opted to do voluntarily just as added precaution. To do all she could do.

"Yes." Everything had come back normal.

"Did you opt to find out the sex of the child?" There'd been no indication in the paperwork she'd shared.

And he wanted to know. Just so he didn't wonder.

"No." She still stood there.

"Is your first ultrasound scheduled?" Sixteen weeks was most common, but some doctors scheduled as early as eight weeks.

She nodded. Sat down, as though understanding now that they weren't quite finished, so he relaxed a bit.

"It's on the twenty-ninth," she added while he sat there, feeling glad that she was willing to give him a bit more of her time.

"You might find out the sex then…" he told her. "But you can tell the technician if you don't want to know. It's not like it's something you're going to be able to ascertain on your own and the tech can keep the information to herself."

She nodded.

That was it. Just a nod.

Did his contract with her allow him to ask about the sex of the child? Was it wrong that he suddenly wanted to know? He could always put in a request at some point. But unless she was willing to share on a regular basis, he had to let time pass before he checked again.

"If you find my next question offensive, feel perfectly comfortable telling me to move on." He waited for her nod before he continued. And noticed that her lips were glossy now, wet from the juice she'd just sipped.

"What led you to the clinic? To this decision?"

At first he thought he'd just earned himself a quick, one-way trip to the door, with the lock turned firmly behind him. Her green-gold eyes seemed to glow for a second there—not in a good way.

"I'm not cut out for having a life partner," she told him. "I struggle just working with my sister in business. In my home…" she said. And then, meeting his gaze, shook her head. "Don't get me wrong. I'm really close to my family. And I have a deep well of love to give. It's just the partner thing…"

"You like to have things your own way. To be the boss in your environment," he guessed, making certain there was understanding, not judgment, in his tone.

"On the contrary," she said, surprising him with a self-deprecating grin. "I feel total responsibility for another person's happiness." She glanced at the flowers again. "I give up myself." And then, looking back at him, added, "Which makes me good parenting material. My child can count on coming first."

"If you've got the right partner, he or she wouldn't let you give up yourself. They'd be watching out for your happiness at the same time." Not that it was any of his business.

"He," she blurted. And then frowned. "I'm attracted to men," she said then.

And he reiterated, though he didn't know why

he was pushing it. "Your abhorrence for a partner might change if you meet the right guy."

She shook her head. "I won't lead you to believe that, even if it makes you feel better. I know myself and I've made my decision. I've been there. I'm not good at it. My mother's the same way and, believe me, my sister and I suffered for it."

Alarm bells went off in his brain. "Suffered how?"

"My stepfather was a drunk. He was actually a pretty cool dad when he wasn't drinking, but when he was…" She shook her head. He wanted to look away. To walk away. He couldn't move.

And not just for his child's sake, though that was part of it.

"Was? Your mother divorced him, then?"

"No. That's the point. Duane always comes first. Over herself and everyone else. She just has this incessant need to please him. And he lets her. He's not narcissistic, really, but he likes her attention."

"Do you still see them?" His gaze was direct.

"Oh, I see where you're going with this," she said, setting her glass on a coaster on the table between them. "And you have no need to worry. In the first place, Duane's been sober for years—of his own accord. And he's been nothing but supportive. He's excited to be a grandfather. He's not an alcoholic and he didn't drink all the time. His work never suffered. He never drank and drove. He drank at home, and was a mean drunk until he lost it on my little sister one Sunday afternoon. He cleared all alcohol out of the house that night and hasn't taken a drink since. Not even a toast of champagne at his niece's wedding. You have no cause to worry here. While he's pragmatic and was strict with us, he was only mean when he was drinking. I don't see him all that much, even though he hasn't said anything out of line in years. And if I ever heard him mouthing off to my child, it would be the last time he saw me or my family."

"So that Sunday, that was the first time he ever got ugly with either of you?"

She wasn't sure what the question had to do with the future well-being of her child. But she didn't mind answering, so said, "Physically, yes. He was never physically abusive, but he'd get really verbally abusive when he was drinking. Mom would just tell us girls to go to our rooms. Or we'd just go there on our own if he ever drank when she wasn't home. That day, though, he'd burst into my sister's room. He'd never done that before. The closed door usually stopped him. For some reason that day it pissed him off."

She couldn't tell by his expression what kind of conclusions he was drawing. And kept telling herself it didn't matter. The minute she said they were done, they were done. Period. She'd kept up her side of the agreement.

But if she wanted him to stay away, to give him the peace of mind to not have to check up on them every few years, she needed to reassure him.

She kind of wanted to reassure him now, anyway. He was a decent guy and she was, overall, a kind woman.

"Angie and I both have scars from growing up with Duane's drunkenness," she said, thinking she could help him understand that her baby was going to be fine with her as a single parent. "Angie more than me, because I never had to face him alone. It was after I left for college that he went off on her. And she hasn't had counseling," she added. Then she got to the point, saying, "My mother loved Duane and gave up herself to him to the point that she couldn't leave him, or make him leave, even when he was being detrimental to our well-being. Now that's not to say that she didn't stick up for us. She did. To a point. She'd take the brunt of his anger. And she'd always insist that he apologize to us afterward, which he always did. He'd say he didn't mean the vile things he'd said. He's spent the past several years proving how sorry he is for the man he'd been when he was drinking. He's sincere. And with all the years of sobriety deserves a second chance. But those words he used to say... don't go away."

You're just like your mother...you don't know when to say no...

She was getting offtrack. The doctor, with his looks of compassion, was easy to talk to. Too easy.

"Anyway, Mom's life wasn't happy. She lived in constant fear of him being invited out with his buddies, or some client. New Year's Eve and Super Bowl Sundays were not good times in our home. All because she couldn't say no. And what I've learned about myself is that I can be similar to her." Just as Duane had always told her.

"How do you know if you don't give yourself a chance to find out?"

More of that blue-eyed dose of caring. The guy was like a feel-good pill.

Like the laces she'd sewn to her plain purse and generic jeans to make herself feel good enough for high school.

"Oh, I had my chance," she told him, taking a long sip of juice. She wasn't really showing yet, but felt bloated and thirsty all the time.

Not something a man would find attractive in a woman he was just meeting.

And that was just fine with her. His gorgeousness and all…that wasn't anything she wanted or needed in her life.

"And I was just like her."

She was an adult now. In control of her life. Making the educated choices that were best for her. And for those she loved.

"I gave up everything that mattered most to me, ditched my loved ones, to please the man I was with and I didn't even see it as a bad thing, at first. You asked about regretting something so much you couldn't let it go?" she asked him. "That's it. Those months of choices I made when I was with Mike, they aren't ever going to happen again. And the only way I can guarantee that is to make certain that I don't ever get that attached to a man again. I've made my choice, Dr. Harmon. No partner. But a happy, healthy family with tons of support."

"Support from whom? What if something happens to you, for instance?"

She had that all taken care of. And told him so. Detailed the arrangements she'd made with Angie. And reiterated the support from other family members and friends.

She had her life back on track.

Craig might be a stop-you-in-your-tracks kind of guy, but he wasn't going to change her mind about doing this alone.

Chapter Seven

He'd donated his sperm so that those who couldn't have a family by traditional means would still be able to have children of their own.

Had he really thought his donation would only be used by married couples who were infertile?

Asking himself the tough questions, in light of Amelia's intimate honesty, Craig was relieved to find that he really wasn't standing in judgment or facing her with preconceived notions. He didn't need his child in a family made up of particular parts, or from a particular financial status. He needed it to be well loved. Secure. Clean and cared for.

Just from his brief looks at Amelia's home, he knew she had the clean part down. The guard who'd kept him from getting upstairs without credentials kind of tended to the secure part. At least in one sense. There was emotional safety to contend with, as well.

With a glance at the folder on the desk, he had as much reassurance as it was possible to get at this point that the woman carrying his child would care for it. The baby was still little more than a fetus and she already had a guy coming to baby-proof her home. Medically she was doing more than necessary. She'd already paid for cord blood storage.

Banking cord blood was a relatively new concept to the general public, but it gave doctors the ability to treat a patient with their own cord blood stem cells—a way to cure some diseases that would otherwise be terminal.

He hadn't even gotten as far as cord blood banking in his thoughts yet, and he was a doctor who'd seen the banked blood save a life.

And as to the child being loved… How did he quantify that?

He'd come to check on the welfare of his unborn seed. He didn't feel…satisfied.

Made more complicated by the fact that he

hadn't counted on being intrigued by the woman carrying that seed.

"Have you dated anyone since your partner died?" Amelia's question gave him a few more minutes just when he'd been struggling with a reason to stay. She'd just finished telling him she wasn't in the market for a relationship—period. So she most definitely wasn't coming on to him.

He could only conclude that she was feeling sorry for him.

Which didn't sit well, either. Yet, there he sat. Not getting up. Getting out. Getting on with his day. His life.

"I have," he told her. "I'm not hard up for a woman, if that's what you're thinking."

"Hardly!" Her burst of incredulity was quickly tempered, but she followed it with, "You're gorgeous. You're a doctor. And you appear to be a genuinely nice guy."

So she'd noticed him. As a man. He felt gratified as he took another sip of juice. Held the glass with one hand, resting it on the palm of the other, which rested on his thigh.

"I was asking whether or not you'd reached the point where you were opening yourself up to another relationship, and possibly a family of your own," she added.

He could pretend to himself that her question was of a personal nature, that she was asking because she was interested in the answer for herself. As if she might consider starting a relationship with him, a bond that could go someplace great. Someplace permanent.

He didn't make that mistake.

"I haven't met anyone who's lasted longer than a few months." A couple had been open to more, but as soon as he'd felt their growing affection, he'd felt compelled to break things off with them. "I'm not out to hurt anyone," he told Amelia. Hoping that she understood that she was included in that statement.

Odd, but it was kind of nice talking to her. A woman who had no interest in him, and yet one with whom he held a deep connection.

"I've had some trouble sleeping since my last contact with Gavin," he told her. "I've had a nightmare or two…nebulous, dark impressions of children screaming and I can't get to them to help them."

He sounded like he needed a shrink. And maybe talking to someone wouldn't hurt.

"I finally concluded that I needed to get this… situation—all of it, not just your part in it—taken care of before I think about having a family of my own," he told her. "The rest is done. You're the last piece."

Probably not his best verbiage, but the way she was watching him, with an open expression, like she was listening and interested, made him think she wasn't taking offense.

"I'm a traditional kind of guy," he told her. "I still believe in marriage and family…sticking together even when the newness wears off. I believe in a love that brings you together, and then, later, keeps you together, in spite of temptations or momentary yearnings for excitement," he admitted, something that he hadn't ever expressed out loud.

She wasn't going to be a part of his life. It made talking about his feelings seem…safer somehow.

"My parents are in their seventies," he told her. "They're still healthy and active, but little things are starting to crop up—one just recently went on a low dose of blood pressure medication, for example—and yet they take things on together. The old saying, two heads are better than one—it's like two lives, joined together, are better than one."

"If you're somehow trying to convince me that my choice to raise this child as a single parent isn't good enough…"

"I'm not." He looked her straight in the eye. "And I apologize. Of course you have no need to know anything about me and I overspoke..." He put his glass on the empty coaster on the table. Time to go. To find a way to get beyond the past and on with his life.

"Oh, no, I'm the one who's sorry." Her words stopped him as he'd been about to stand. "Seriously." She shook her head. "I have a tendency to get defensive," she continued. "Probably comes from knowing that you have to watch your own back. And...funny that you should mention my need to know something about you..."

Her words ended midstream and she was looking at him as though sizing him up for some kind of project.

His curiosity was piqued.

And he wasn't sure that was a good thing.

Craig Harmon was a genuinely nice man. The impression came home to her again. More and more she was getting the impression that he really was no threat to her at all—as he kept asserting.

But all of his talk about family, about tradition— she believed he was being sincere. She believed him.

He was doing everything he could to reassure her that she had nothing to fear from him. Her life, her choices, were anything but traditional. He didn't want her. Or her child.

Just as she had her life plans, he had his. The complete antithesis of hers.

And he had no need to take what she had, even if he could. He wanted to fall in love. Get married. And have children traditionally with his wife.

She wanted to do what she could to give him peace of mind. One person to another. She'd be a jerk not to want that. They weren't just biological components. Even Angie would agree, would want her to do the right thing. To show some of the compassion she was sometimes too quick to feel where others were concerned.

Her sister was even more of a bleeding heart than she was.

"I never knew my father," she said clearly, turning in her chair, one foot pulled up with her, as she faced him more directly. It was scary, opening up to him. And yet, felt good, too. With their pre-established boundaries—he was a safe place. "It was hard sometimes, growing up, not knowing who I came from. Not knowing if some of my traits were his. So…since you're here, it seems kind of a nice idea for me to know a bit about you, whatever you want to share…so that I can fill in the blanks for my son or daughter someday, when the questions come. I'm fully aware they inevitably will."

He lifted his ankle across the opposite knee, his forearms relaxing against the sides of the chair, seeming to take a silent assessment of her.

And she had a second to understand how she must have been making him feel—wondering whether or not to trust. Looking for ulterior motives?

Or was that just her?

And why did she care?

"Does your father know you exist?"

"I lived with him for the first year of my life. I don't remember him. And my mother...my sister and I never mentioned him to her. Not ever. It upset her too much."

"Did he die?"

"No." She didn't need to get into that.

"You said your sister, Angeline, is a year younger than you."

He'd learned that when she'd told him about her sister's involvement with the baby, that Angeline was the child's legal guardian and held medical and legal power of attorney were anything to happen to Amelia.

"Right."

"So...do you share a biological father?"

"Yes."

He watched her, making her think of an examining room and allowing the doctor to diagnose what ailed her.

She didn't need his diagnosis.

But didn't seem to mind the questions. Maybe she should, but she didn't. Should she be worried about that?

"Your father left when your sister was born?"

"So, technically, I misspoke," she said, simply because his gaze required the truth. "I didn't actually live with him the first year of my life. He was in the picture. He moved out shortly after my mom found out she was pregnant with Angie." Might just as well get it over with. Personal questions weren't her fave, but she understood his need to know more. He wasn't going to be in his child's life, this man who'd already lost a son to a system that didn't seem just. Knowing the details of the life of the woman who'd be raising the child would be a comfort to him. She hoped.

Although her job wasn't to comfort him…

"I was a little over three months old. He and Mom had been high school sweethearts. They'd married shortly after graduation and then I came along that first year. He thought it was cool at first, when it was all new and they were making great plans. But when reality set in, he wasn't ready for the responsibility." All according to her mother—the only source she had to go on.

Like Angie coming along so soon after Amelia. Her mother would have known better than to have unprotected sex when her baby was still so little. But "the father," as they'd called him between the two of them, had probably been looking for what he needed and she wouldn't have denied him. Or stopped him long enough to protect herself.

Margaret had been breastfeeding Amelia and back then there hadn't been a birth control pill you could take and still safely nurse.

"He moved in with a buddy of his for a time, but still apparently came by and took care of things at the house, mowed the grass, paid his share of the bills."

And those six months of contribution had given Margaret hope, undying, constricting hope that he'd be back. She'd watched that hope eat her mother alive. Had somehow known, even as a young girl listening to her mother talk about her dad, that her mother wasn't seeing everything straight.

"After Angie was born he left the state. Took a job on a pipeline and never looked back. Never sent a dime. Never contacted her again."

"What about child support?"

"Mom never went after him for it. She wanted him to be free to do what he needed to do. She didn't want to fight with him. She married Duane when I was ten, and once he was in the picture, my father's name was never to be mentioned. It's like he never existed. Mom fully supported Duane's stance and wouldn't answer us if we ever asked anything. She'd rebuke us instead, reminding us that Duane was supporting us and that we needed to respect him and abide by his wishes."

She heard the small bite of bitterness in her voice. And took it as a warning to not let the past rob her future. She was her mother's daughter, but she wasn't going to make her same choices. Her same mistakes.

Mike's infidelity had been a blessing, so she left before they were married and had had kids who would suffer. After all of those years of Christmases spent with a mother who always kidded herself that "this year" was the one that their dad would be back, having to stay close to home so they didn't miss him, she hadn't been willing to forgive Mike and take him back. To "love" him enough. To be "understanding" enough.

"Now that you're an adult, have you ever tried to find your father?"

She shook her head slowly. So oddly comfortable sharing things with him that she normally never talked about. And again she wondered if she should be concerned. Was this just for him? "Angie did, though." She continued to answer questions that belonged inside a family.

"Was she successful?"

"Depends on your definition of success." She shrugged. Hugged her shin. "She found him. In Alaska. He's captain of a fishing boat that spends months out at sea at a time. He asked why she was contacting him. What she wanted from him. Made it very clear he had no interest in her, and had nothing for her to get from him. They had the one phone conversation and that was it."

"Did he ask about you or your mom?"

Funny how this man was sensitive enough to come up with that question. And maybe that was why she was talking to him. Because he really listened—beyond words.

"No."

She didn't blame "the father." Not really. She just learned from him. From both of her parents. Angie had started her search for their father after the incident with Duane. During the time when Amelia had been all in with Mike and virtually ignoring the rest of her loved ones. Letting them all down. Angie had been devastated by their father's response to her call.

"This is why I'm not going to risk putting a child of mine through that," she told him. "Just like I'm not going to be trapped by love into having to live with a man who makes me unhappy. Angie and I have felt abandoned our entire lives, but it was kind of a nebulous sort of thing there, not tragic, you know? A part of us, but not completely defining us. But after that phone call…"

Angie hadn't called her, but after finding out that Mike had slept with some woman he'd met in a bar a short time later, Amelia had gone home for the weekend.

And after those two days with her sister, she'd gone back to college, ended things with Mike and put herself in counseling.

"So…in a way, this is really good," she told Craig, nodding. Smiling. "My baby will not only know that I wanted him or her so badly that I purposely, knowingly and consciously, chose every aspect of her birth, but that her biological component cared enough to make certain that she was being born into a loving, secure home."

Yes, it was all wrapping up rather neatly. Or so she hoped.

Chapter Eight

"Oh!"

Craig glanced over at Amelia, as she half gasped, and put her hand to her lower stomach. Immediately on alert, he assessed her skin color, her pupils. "What?" he asked, reaching a hand automatically to where hers was touching her abdomen.

"Excuse me!" she said, pushing his hand away. "I had a…cramp…" She looked away, off the balcony, and he followed suit.

What in the hell was he doing, touching her?

And how could it possibly have felt like the sun had come out inside him?

"If you're cramping..." He leaned toward her again, and asked, "Do you mind if I just...feel your pulse?"

Flinging her arm out, she looked away again, and didn't flinch when his hand wrapped around the warm skin at her wrist. He concentrated on even rhythm. Counting. Gave himself the chance to remember who he was and what he was there for. And noting, at the same time, that her pulse was a tad fast.

"It was just...you know...indigestion type," she said when Craig dropped her wrist. He tried to forget he'd put his hand on her stomach. Tried to forget how much he'd liked it there.

"Is everything okay, doctor?" She was smiling. And putting him at ease. Telling him she understood he hadn't been hitting on her. That it was okay.

"Steady pulse, perfect rhythm," he told her, leaving out the fast pace part. It had already slowed by the time he was letting go. Which told him the increased rate had most likely been due to his touch.

"So, do you have any more questions?"

She wasn't kicking him out. Something had just happened between them and he was still there. If questions were what was keeping them together, what was allowing them to be comfortable spending time together, he could come up with a whole lot more.

"If your mother had been willing to tell you about your dad, what questions would you have asked? What did you feel like you needed to know?" Feeling renewed energy, and a sense of reaching for a future where he was at peace, Craig gave the woman carrying his child an encouraging smile. Told himself it was just all about the baby, but he wasn't completely buying it.

But for the next hour, he answered her questions. At one point she asked if she could take notes.

Eventually, long after both of their glasses of juice were empty, Amelia invited him to her kitchen where she'd put together a couple of onion, cucumber and grilled chicken wraps, with some kind of dressing she'd made out of mayonnaise, vinegar and mustard, that he could see—she'd had him out on the paved and walled room-size balcony manning the grill—and they'd sat outside with some muted lighting she'd turned on, eating dinner together. Two blocks of the city lay before them, and then, in the distance, the ocean's vastness.

He felt like he was on a luxurious vacation—and appreciated her ability to make home feel that way.

And still, after the dishes were rinsed and in the washer, he accepted her invitation for an after-dinner drink—his coffee, hers decaffeinated green tea—back out on the balcony.

He didn't feel like he was done yet. And though he knew he should be, he continued to sit with her. To enjoy watching her as she spoke. Sitting there with her, knowing she was pregnant with his child, he had a sense of family he'd never really known with Tricia. Which made no sense to him.

Amelia's phone had rung a time or two—she'd let it go to voicemail, but sent a text. He wondered who she was close to, besides her sister. Who'd be calling her on a Saturday evening. Had a moment of discomfort when he considered that it could be a man who was interested in her. Just because she wasn't looking for a partner didn't mean she didn't date. And he had to get home to Talley.

"Thank you," Amelia said to him as they sat gazing out over the city. "This was really nice. You've been incredibly patient and kind, answering all of these questions."

She sounded sated. Not just satisfied. Sated. He wondered at the distinction his mind was making.

Felt something significant there.

"It's you doing me the favor," he reminded her. "Your questions tell me a lot about you, about what mattered to you as a kid, what matters to you now, and so…what kind of parent you'll most likely be." She'd been looking at him, but glanced away. "Besides," he added, "you're easy to talk to."

The words brought her gaze back to him. He wanted to hold on to it.

"You're easy to talk to, too," she surprised him by saying. "I've told you things I don't ever talk about. About my dad. And Mike."

"Your ex."

She nodded. Glanced out again, and then back. "He was unfaithful to me," she said. "After insisting that I be 'all in' with him—that I put him and our life together first, above all else—he slept with someone else."

Anger flared for a second, that someone would treat a decent human being, let alone Amelia, that way… He paused, reining in feelings that generally didn't ever get out of check.

"Sounds like the guy had self-esteem issues," he said. What was with him that night? You'd think he'd specialized in psychology rather than just taking the requisite classes for his medical degree. "And was a first-class idiot," he added.

His voice had softened, and when he heard that, he knew he wasn't just sitting there for peace of mind.

The long look she gave him, the softening around her eyes, drew him.

"I'm pretty sure I've blamed myself in about every way possible," she slowly admitted. "Mostly, though, I hate that I didn't know. I eventually found out, thinking, when I caught him in the act, that it was the first time, but then discovered that it had been going on for weeks. While he'd been sleeping with me."

Leaning on the arm of his padded wrought iron chair, he put his face closer to hers, letting the darkness soften the intimacy of the movement. "He was a fool, Amelia," he told her, his voice low, but deadly serious. "A decent man would know what a gem he had in you, in your devotion, and he'd cherish that, protect it," he told her.

He had no idea why she'd been exposed to the dregs of the male gender, but needed her to know that not all men had a horrible side. That many would be worthy of her trust.

She didn't say anything. Just sat there, looking at him. A minute passed and then she slowly turned toward the lights bobbing on the ocean in the far distance.

An idea occurred to him. But it was one that could lose him any ground he'd built with her. Glancing at her, he considered the wisdom of holding his counsel, leaving things to end on a good note.

Unless…

"Would it be awful if you and I were to remain in contact?" he proposed. "Not in any way that changes things. That child is all yours. I have no say. No rights. Period. But what if I was around, just a background figure who could look out for her health and happiness? What if she knows me just as a casual friend of yours? Someone you all see once in a while. Someone who, if the need ever arose, would be there to help in a time of crisis, someone he or she knows and can trust?"

His feet slid into place to stand as he voiced the question in its various forms. He was braced to stand. To follow the instructions he was sure would follow: to leave her home and not contact her any time soon.

When she said nothing, he remained braced.

"Do you have a bike?" he asked, many silent seconds later, just to fill the silence.

"What?" She turned to look at him, frowning, as though she'd just joined their little gathering.

As though she'd been deep in thought? He'd give his small fortune to know what she'd been thinking.

"A bike? Do you own a bike?"

"I used to. Not anymore."

"Biking is a good, low-impact exercise," he dropped into the night.

"Okaayyy."

"I've still got Tricia's bike…"

He was walking a tightrope, not sure where it led. Not sure it wouldn't be better if he just fell off and was done.

He didn't want that to happen.

"I could pick you up tomorrow, say around two, and we could go for a quick easy ride on Ellory Road."

The quiet, mostly flat, gently curving two-mile stretch wound through an upscale neighborhood with homes that all sat on at least an acre of grassy and wooded lots. Because it was zoned residential, the speed limit was slow. And the traffic was minimal.

"I haven't agreed to your suggestion that we stay in contact."

"You haven't disagreed." He had to point it out.

"I know."

He glanced at her and found her looking at him.

"Why not?" he asked, thinking they might be crossing into new territory. Into a place where they might be more than casual acquaintances.

And then he remembered her adamant desire

to remain single; he wasn't going to change her mind on that one. Knew that it wasn't even right of him to try—all baby considerations aside. Just as he knew that he wasn't going to change his mind about wanting to get married and stay that way for the rest of his life.

"Because I'm afraid that no matter how I feel, it might be best for my baby if you *are* a casual acquaintance in his or her life," she said.

And his heart skidded to a halt.

Chapter Nine

What in the hell was she thinking, making that statement to Craig about having him be an acquaintance in her baby's life? She wasn't thinking.

Meeting her sister for breakfast the next morning at an upscale bagel shop down by the mostly private stretch of beach in town, Amelia straightened her shoulders and went inside.

Angie had already ordered and had their bagels and tea at a high-top table for two by the window. Noting her sister's black leggings, long fluted white blouse, makeup and matching black-and-white earrings in all three piercings, she took a deep breath. Angie always dressed more formally when she was upset. Like the clothes gave her strength. And maybe they did, if they made her feel better about herself.

She knew she should have called Angie back the night before, rather than just texting to set up a breakfast meet, but Craig had been sitting there, he'd touched her stomach, taken her pulse, warmed her from the inside out. She'd needed time to collect her thoughts.

And it had been after nine when Craig had left and she hadn't wanted the questions that would come from her sister if she'd called that late. Better for Angie to think she'd gone to bed early to catch up on the sleep she'd missed that week with the intercontinental travel.

Pregnancy required more sleep, too.

Leaning over to kiss her sister's cheek, and to receive Angie's return greeting, Amelia stepped up to take a seat on her stool.

"I saw Craig Harmon," she said, putting it right out there. Honesty was the only way to even have a chance of winning back the deep level of trust Angie had once had in her.

Her sister's sudden ashen face broke her heart a little more. Nerves that had already been iffy started to tense and create churning inside as she considered what might come.

Before Angie could say anything, if she'd even been going to say anything, Amelia told her sister about her sperm donor's visit. About his desire to marry. His understanding of and respect for her own personal choice to remain single.

She told Angie about the man's honest need for peace of mind, where his sperm donation was concerned, waiting for Angie's compassion to take over from whatever insecurities she might be feeling.

"He doesn't want any control over this baby," she told her sister, who'd yet to touch her tea or bagel. Or say a word. "He just needs to know that it's okay."

More than just okay, but in the moment, the word sufficed.

"You like him." Angie's words fell like rocks on her chest.

"No, sweetie, I don't." She might have, pre-Mike. Who was she kidding? She could see her old self swooning if the doctor had asked her out. He was gorgeous. And, even better, not afraid to talk about feelings. "I can't," she told her. "Those impulsive feelings…they're dead to me." She hadn't realized fully until the night before when, though she found Craig Harmon as hot as they came, she hadn't been tempted to throw caution to the wind and ask him to bed. Which was what she'd done when she first met Mike.

"I learned my lesson, Angie. I know myself, and it's like the knowing brought with it an internal safety net. I think about being in a relationship and I just shut down. I truly don't want it."

No more living with the constant worry of having to please. No more putting her happiness in the control of one person. Or giving up self to make someone else happy. Or having the light in her life suddenly change hue and not be alight at all.

Studying her, Angie picked up her bagel. Took a bite. Seemed to see what she needed to find in Amelia's gaze as she chewed and then nodded.

"It would be easier for me to accept this if you'd told me ahead of time that you were going to see him," she mentioned as she took another bite of bagel.

Not really hungry, but knowing she needed her energy, especially in light of the afternoon activity she had planned, Amelia followed suit. She ate half her bagel before she said anything more.

"You're right." She finally acknowledged what she'd known from the beginning. "But I knew what you'd think, Angie, and I had to prove to you that you were wrong. I had to see him and be okay so you'd know that I am."

Reaching for Amelia's hand, Angie gave it a squeeze. "You know that I don't think you fall for the first guy who gives you a second look, right?"

"Of course I do. In the first place, I'd be falling all over the place," she joked.

"But this guy…he's not just some guy," Angie said. "I can tell you're attached to him already, Mel. And that *is* something you could lose yourself over."

She didn't say a word.

Couldn't.

Because she'd come to her sister to discuss the idea of maintaining contact with Craig, on a peripheral level. She needed Angie's unbiased opinion on the matter.

And had a feeling Angie wasn't capable of giving it to her.

They had their issues.

"That's the only reason I got scared. And because you kept it from me, like there was something to hide…" She held up a hand when Amelia started to speak. "I know. I understand why you saw him first. I'm not saying it was the wrong thing to do, only explaining why I—"

"I know," Amelia said, understanding and agreeing all in the same two words.

Amelia wasn't going to live her life to please

others. And yet, was she doing just that with Angie? She had to do what she thought was right. And if Angie was ever going to be able to trust her implicitly again, she had to be honest with her. But not at the expense of her own life.

She turned the talk to business for a few minutes. One of their most expensive embossers had gone down at the factory the night before. It was back up and running, but they'd lost an hour of production time. She was the partner on call that weekend. They discussed adjustments they could make to the schedule, putting a bigger run on hold and moving up a critical, smaller job, and while Angie finished her bagel, Amelia put a call in to the production manager who was at the factory that morning, giving the order to make the change.

"I had an email from Hermine," Angie said, mentioning the male designer she'd met with that past week. He had a new line that he thought would be made perfect with Feel Good embellishments, and if the paperwork looked as good as the man made his offer sound, they'd be signing with him.

"He sent the contract?" she asked.

"No, although he said his lawyer will have it to Tanya early in the week. He was writing to offer me a job. I did a couple of drawings when I met with him, made some small changes to a couple of his designs, and he thinks I'd make a great addition to his team." Angie's tone was light. She was smiling.

And still, Amelia's entire being constricted. "Is it something you want to consider?" she had to ask. And was afraid to ask. She didn't want Angie to go. But knew she had to support her sister if that was what she really wanted.

Just as Angie was supporting her.

"Of course not!" Angie looked her straight in the eye. "You know that Feel Good, you and me, family, mean everything to me. Besides, I'd have to move to New York and there's no way I want be that far away from mom. Or the girls," she added, referring to her friends.

Relieved beyond words that Angie was as happy where she was as Amelia had assumed, she still needed to be sure. "What about the work, Angie? You've always loved the artistic part of what we do most. Would you like to spend all your time working on designs, rather than like it is now, with both of us spending far more time on the business end?"

Of course, if Angie would be okay with expanding Feel Good, of taking a chance and bringing on more top people to handle the business end of things, they could both spend more time designing. And then be able to produce more products to sell, too.

"I do love designing," Angie said, pausing for a second with a smile on her face. "But truthfully, I love being in charge, too." Her little sister's grin was all sass then, and Amelia chuckled.

They both liked being in charge. She figured they came by that honestly, having grown up feeling as though they had control over nothing.

"So...tell me about Craig Harmon. Do you feel good about his genetic contribution to our little one there?" Angie sobered, sitting back with her teacup in hand. Her sister's more classically beautiful face was unlined, her gaze clear and caring as she met Amelia's gaze.

She wanted to be as open and free to talk to Angie as her younger sister needed her to be. And she hesitated, on edge, nerves clamoring in every part of her body.

If she said too much, Angie might think she really *liked* the guy. Which she did. But on a casual basis only, which her sister wasn't likely to believe.

And if she didn't say enough, Angie would think she was holding back.

Having a sibling as close as she and Angie were was a godsend. By far the absolute best blessing in her life.

And it was hard, too, having someone know you well enough to be able to complete your thoughts for you.

And then stand in judgment on them if she thought you were going to hurt herself.

"I feel as good about his genetic contribution now as I did when I chose him," she said, searching for total honesty, if not a full disclosure that could easily be misconstrued. "He seems like a decent guy from a decent family. Middle of the line, you know. Not obsessed about anything, like totally into any one thing, and yet proficient at many things. They're educated, of course, but we already knew that, or knew that *he* was at least. They have good teeth, no major illnesses in the family and no mental illnesses of which he was aware."

"Does he have siblings?"

"No."

"Does he seem close with his parents?"

"Yes."

"Does he like pets?"

"Yes."

"Has he ever been married?"

"No."

When Angie's lower lip pushed outward, Amelia's spirits shot down to the floor. She knew that look.

"You asked him about his marital status?"

"Yes. If he had a wife, she would have been in-volved in the conversation." No, that wasn't quite how it had gone. He'd said if she had a husband he should be involved in the conversation. "Or maybe he just told me," she added, feeling as though she was floundering now in a dark mass of seaweed.

"He told me," she said, trying to keep Angie worry free and keep herself honest at the same time. "He was telling me about his reasons for seeking me out in the first place. Like I told you, his partner had been killed..."

"That didn't mean he'd never been married."

No, it didn't. And she sure as hell wasn't going to tell her sister about the man's biggest desire being a wife and family, one wife for the rest of his life.

For a long time she'd believed her mom, that their father would be coming home. When they'd been little enough to play house they used to pre-tend that, every single time, their dad was home, and mention of him wouldn't make their mother cry. It wasn't until her mother had started dating Duane that Amelia had realized that her daddy wasn't coming back to them. She'd been in third grade. That had been a tough year.

"He and Tricia were together from the time he graduated," she said now. "And before that he'd shared an apartment with another medical student, a guy from here," she added. "Here being Marie Cove. And I know this because his roommate's mother works at the Parent Portal and that's how he ended up getting involved with artificial insemination to begin with. A choice he now regrets. As I told you."

She was overcompensating. She heard it happening.

"What?" she asked, noticing Angie's frown. She had nothing to feel guilty for. Other than decisions of the past. And the fact that she hadn't told her sister she was seeing Craig the night before—and that one was arguable.

"I'm confused. You saw him, at his request, so that he could learn enough about you to put his mind at ease about the well-being of the baby…"

"Right."

"They why do *you* know so much about *him*?"

Because he'd been easy to talk to. Because they'd talked for hours. Because she'd made him dinner. Because she'd wanted to know.

He'd listened, really listened, without judgment… and had offered comment that rang true to her.

Because what she'd said, felt, experienced in her life, seemed to matter. It hadn't just been all about what he needed.

All of which meant nothing other than that they were two human beings with something in common, being kind to each other.

But Angie wasn't going to believe that.

"You're attracted to him." Angie's tone had lowered. And then she stood. "You're trying to hide it from me."

Amelia stood, too. "Angie, please…"

"Answer me this, then…"

Nodding, Amelia waited, eager for the opportunity to show her sister that she was on top of things.

"Are you seeing him again?"

A lie was on the tip of her tongue. She hoped to God she hadn't been about to utter it. Either way she never got the chance.

"You are!" Angie said, her voice raised enough that the pair of women seated closest to their table glanced over at them. "You're seeing him again."

She didn't know what to say. Not standing there in a coffee shop.

"You're her!" Angie said, pushing her way past a stool in her path. "You're just like Mom!"

More people heard her than just the two women next to them. Other than a peripheral vision realization, Amelia didn't bother checking to see who, or how many. Her eyes were focused on her sister's back as Angie walked out on her. She was pregnant, attempting to build a family, and it seemed to be fracturing in front of her very eyes instead.

Chapter Ten

"Angie!" Chasing after her sister on the beach, Amelia called out to her a second time. Angie didn't stop. Didn't even slow down. Until, half a mile down from where they'd parked their cars, Angie suddenly dropped to the sand in her nice clothes, sitting with her legs up, her arms wrapped around them, staring out to the ocean.

Other people milled around.

Angie's cheeks were wet. Two small streams still trickled down them.

"Angie... I swear to you...,"

The woman shook her head of long, fire-red hair, strands sticking to the tears on her face.

"I'm so sorry, Mel." She turned as Amelia dropped down beside her, the sand cold and hard against the butt of the leggings she had on, in preparation for bike riding that she might or might not be doing that afternoon.

If she couldn't make this right with Angie, she wasn't going.

"What are you sorry for?" she asked, genuinely confused.

"For what I said back there. About you being like Mom."

The words had stung, particularly coming from her sister, but… "They're true," she said with a shrug.

"Yeah, in some ways," Angie said, turning to look at her, her expression almost fierce. "But I said it like Duane used to, like it's a bad thing, and it's not, Mel. You've got her best qualities. Her compassion. Her loyalty. Her determination to love fiercely."

Love *stupidly*. *Unhealthily*, she silently corrected.

"I just… I can't believe I just…it's like I heard Duane's words in my brain, mixed in with panic and just spewed them." Angie shook her head. "I can't believe I did that." She turned to Amelia again. "I'm just so sorry. That I would…me… I'm the last…"

"It's okay." Love flowed through Amelia as she put an arm around her sister. "He said a helluva lot worse things to me. And coming from you, no matter the tone, they don't mean what they did coming from him."

Angie nodded. Took her hand, and turned to face her. "But what if I meant them?" she almost whispered. They were far enough up from the water that the surf was like white noise in the distance. And in January, there wasn't as much marine life around as there would be in a few months. Amelia thought about sand crabs for a moment. And then tides. She took a deep breath and reminded herself that she would always be okay. No matter what.

"I didn't mean to spew them," Angie finally said, her tone soft. As sweet as ever. Sorry. "I didn't even mean to say them. But…"

"You aren't wrong," Amelia couldn't bear to leave her sister hanging there, feeling awful for speaking the truth. "I *am* like her. Which is why I've made the life decisions I've made."

Angie knew this. They'd talked about it.

But knowing and believing were two very different things.

"I'm not kidding around here, Ang. Or keeping a door open. There's not even a crack in a window," she added, panicking for a moment when she thought of the rush of attraction she'd felt for Craig Harmon. Several times the night before. All the guy had to do was say something that reached inside her and she'd melted.

But she'd never left her seat. Never even thought about doing so.

Because she couldn't.

"I have to be accountable to what I know about myself. Just like Duane has to keep himself out of the bars with his friends."

"He went to one yesterday for lunch," Angie said. "Which is why I stayed in Santa Barbara so long. I had to make certain he came home sober."

Sitting cross-legged now, her knees touching Angie's as they sat like twins in the sand, facing each other, Amelia asked, "And?"

Angie's nod sent relief flooding through her. For their mother's sake. "He was dry as could be. It was kind of awkward, though," she added. "He knew why I'd stayed, and instead of just letting it go, he looked straight at me and thanked me for loving my mother that much. And then told me that he wasn't even tempted to take a sip of alcohol, and hadn't been since…that day. He said…it…haunts him and any time he envisions himself holding even a bottle of beer, he gets a sick feeling inside."

Mouth hanging open, Amelia stared at her. "He *said* that?"

"I know, weird, huh?"

Duane had written a letter of apology to Angeline. And to Amelia, too, shortly after that horrible day. He'd made a brief mention of being sorry for anything he might have said drunk over the years that could have been hurtful. If he'd been able to remember any of those incidents, he hadn't said so. The apology had rung hollow to Amelia. His words rang clearly in her mind—and he should know them. Own them. Anything less wasn't enough.

But she let it be. And he hadn't said an unkind word to either her or Angie since he quit drinking.

He'd been a jerk drunk, but sober, he'd provided for them, even when they'd been growing up. He'd helped them with homework. Attended some school functions. He hadn't always understood them. Had often not agreed with them. But he'd tried a lot of the time.

Angie glanced down at the sand and then back up at Amelia. "Why are you seeing him again?"

They weren't talking about Duane anymore.

"You remember how it felt when we were little

and we found out 'the father' really wasn't coming back, like Mom had always said?"

Angie nodded. "And the nights we'd sit up and talk about what he was like. Wondering where he was… And if he had red hair like mine," Angie said, a note of bitterness in her tone. They knew now that he did because Angie had asked, but he hadn't cared a bit to know that Angie had his hair.

"But more, think of how horrible it felt those times we got ourselves scared that he wasn't coming back because of us. That he'd abandoned *us*, not Mom. Do you remember?"

The question was completely rhetorical. Angie nodded, anyway. "But this is different," she said. "The baby will know that a father didn't leave him or her."

"I know, but I also know that I always wondered, since I am like Mom—I wondered what 'the father' was like. To know if I had some of his good qualities that were equally compelling…"

"We're all a combination of the genes that created us," she said, hoping so strongly that her sister could understand. "If we can give this baby a fuller sense of self…"

Her sister's hazel gaze pinned hers. She put her heart into that shared silent communication. Her heart and a promise, too. "He wants to get married and have his own family, Angie. He doesn't want ours. But he's a man who spends his life trying to save lives. A man who's watching the boy he'd raised fall into a bad way. He's only asking to look out for my baby's health and happiness. The very same things we want for it. He doesn't want to be part of our lives. To spend time with the baby or attend functions. He isn't asking to be considered at any decision times. He only wants to be present enough to ease the way if he can while he lives his own life, with his own family."

Her sister didn't look away, and Amelia took a deep breath. "He wants to meet you, Ang. He knows that you're the baby's legal guardian if anything were to happen to me, and he just wants to reassure you that he's not going to get in our way."

"You told him about me?"

"Of course I did. You're a large part of the plan here, especially when it comes to security for this little one."

Concern shone from every nuance of Angie's presence.

"When are you going to see him again?"

"This afternoon." Only to exercise. Her sister wasn't going to believe that, though.

"This afternoon? As in Saturday night and Sunday afternoon? Two dates in the same weekend?"

She looked away, stopped talking as she heard her voice rise. When she turned back, her tone was still shaky, but laced with kindness. "You're scaring me."

"You're scaring yourself," Amelia had to point out, able to remain calm because she knew the truth. "You're imagining what you fear coming true, rather than hearing truth in what I'm telling you."

"But what if you're lying to yourself, Mel?"

Angie knew how to hit at her biggest fear, of course. And seemed to have a penchant for doing so—something she'd like to mention, but didn't.

"I'm not."

Angie nodded again, but Amelia knew her sister wasn't convinced.

Not yet.

But she would be.

Time would tell.

The bike he had for her was blue, Amelia noted as she got out of her car and walked toward him. They'd met at a fruit market not far from the neighborhood where they'd be riding, Craig pulling both machines down one at a time from a rack on the top of his SUV. He slung them around as though they were grocery bags, setting his sleek black men's ten-speed up on its kickstand and then settling hers beside it.

The bike had a compact crankset, which meant twenty gears, he'd told her the night before. While she'd loved to ride when she was in high school, that was mostly to get out of the house and clear her head, and he'd assured her that she'd do just fine with Tricia's ten-speed. It was all a foreign language to her, but she wanted to give it—and being around *him*—a try.

Regular exercise would not only make her delivery easier, but it would lessen her recovery time, as well, which was why she'd already started a low-impact regime at a local gym. With a business to run, she couldn't afford to take weeks and weeks away from the office recovering from childbirth.

The gym work was boring her so much she dreaded going. Which was why she'd eventually accepted Craig's offer of a bike to use. Which was exactly what she'd told him when she'd finally given him her answer.

"Here's a water for you," he said as she approached, offering her a plastic bottle that was sweating from the cold liquid inside.

"I'm good," she told him, avoiding looking directly at him. The sight of the man in riding gear—long tight black pants—was…completely unexpected. "I've got one here." She forced the words, turning to show him the bottle resting against her lower back, held there by the belt strapped around her waist. He couldn't see the belt from the front because of the T-shirt she was wearing on top of her leggings. And when she was turned around she couldn't see him.

Or that…bulge.

Her heart thumped and she wet her lips.

The water-bottle belt was new. As were the black-and-white-and-silver tennis shoes she'd picked up after bagels with her sister.

Amelia knew she didn't do anything in half measures.

A trait she got from "the father"? Assuming he had at least one good one?

Get a woman pregnant, not once but twice, and then not just leave her, but do it without warning, without any means of support forever.

Shaking her head, she listened as Craig told her about the bike's gears. A little different from the ten-speed she remembered, but enough the same that she knew what she was doing.

"Let me know if I go too fast," he told her as they mounted their bikes, and she wanted to nod vigorously. To just put it out there and tell him, *Yes.* Yes to having him in her life, looking like that—

it was too fast and too much. Way too much. "We want aerobic exercise," he said, mentioning heart rate information that she already knew.

Clearly the man wasn't at all affected by her thighs showing at the bottom of the long-sleeved and long-bodied T-shirt she'd worn to cover up ass…ets.

"You want to stay in good physical shape, but now is not the time to push yourself."

Yeah, she knew, but nodded, anyway. And again when he asked if she'd eaten breakfast and lunch.

Yep, she'd eaten. With Angie. Who would be having apoplexy if she could see her right now, re-acting to that bulge in those biker pants as though she'd never seen a man's penis area clearly delin-eated before.

He handed her a helmet. Put his on. And asked if she'd taken her vitamins, and she nodded again, too het up to get defensive about his invasiveness.

She'd have stopped him if he'd pulled out a stethoscope or tried to check her vitals. She wasn't his patient, but as they set off, helmets on heads, it kind of felt like he was just another medical person on the team who was helping her bring a healthy baby into the world. The trainer at the Par-ent Portal, for instance, was one. She'd met with the woman once. Took down all the necessary information and had pretty much followed her suggestions, too. She'd just been bored to death at the gym.

So yeah, the bike riding, Craig and his questions…it was all just part of the medical process.

Did men wear cups when they rode bikes? The question, brought on by that brief glimpse of bulge she couldn't get out of her head, made her miss the pedal as they started out. Had to start a second time, her hands a little shaky on the low handlebar grips.

Concentrating on staying upright was a godsend. Let her catch her breath. And get her sanity back.

She stayed far enough behind him that there was no chance for conversation. Partially on purpose. Partially because she was regaining her bike riding confidence and her decorum.

The first time she glanced ahead, she almost lost all confidence, and her balance, as well. The sight of his backside in those pants, as Craig sat half-bent over to steer his bike, seemed to have some invisible cord attached to the seat she was on, sending electric shock waves to her crotch.

Jeezy Pete. It wasn't like she hadn't had sex before. A lot. As recently as the previous summer when she'd had a fun fling with a recently divorced lawyer friend of Tanya's. She'd enjoyed the sex. And him.

There'd been no electricity.

She couldn't actually remember a time when there had been, but those things came and went. One didn't always commit them to memory.

Half a block from their cars, they entered an elite neighborhood. Craig swiped a card at a locked gate to enter.

He lived there? He'd never mentioned that he was taking her to ride in his own neighborhood. Not that it mattered, really.

Just seemed…a little too personal.

"Why not just have me meet you at your place so you didn't have to pack up the bikes?" she asked when they stopped together.

"Because I don't intend to take you to my place," he said, glancing sideways to look at her. "Correct me if I'm wrong, but I got the impression you'd think that too personal."

He wasn't wrong.

She was grateful that he was sensitive enough to have picked up on that.

And acted upon it, too.

Maybe it wouldn't be completely foolish to relax a little bit.

Maybe.

Chapter Eleven

The woman carrying his baby was far too unique to live life alone. Someone was being cheated out of an intriguing, somewhat frustrating, savvy and caring mate. Okay, he could see that he'd at least like a shot at perhaps being that someone...but also understood that Amelia didn't want a partner.

He even understood why.

It just didn't seem right. For her, more than anyone. She took on so much by herself. Because she feared her inability to love in a healthy way. As Craig had the thought, he knew that just because something seemed wrong, life still let it happen. Like a child with a leukemia diagnosis. A thirty-seven-year-old dropping dead of an aneurysm. A wealthy mother being killed in a car accident and leaving her young son orphaned and vulnerable to the father who'd never wanted him, but wanted his money. A woman spending her entire life in love with a man married to another family.

A father walking out on his high school sweetheart and their two infants, and throwing away his second chance when one of the daughters contacted him almost two decades later.

He'd slowed his ride once they were inside the gated community and she eventually rode up beside him.

"This is so great," she told him. "Just so peaceful, and yet, with that little bit of breeze against your skin… I'd forgotten how calming I used to find it, riding my bike."

Calming. He glanced her way, surprised she'd used that word. He rode to find his peace. Always had.

She glanced at him and their bikes almost collided. Straightening her wheel, she said, "I imagine this is boring for you. I feel bad, slowing your pace."

"I ride slow sometimes," he told her. "You see more that way."

They rounded a corner. Were on his street. A

couple of blocks from his property. Which meant about four houses, all set back on their acres of greenery with the mature trees standing in the front yards. The first time he'd seen Tricia's house he'd known he'd wanted to own it with her. Or, as it turned out, buy it *from* her.

It was the perfect family home. Like something on the cover of a home design magazine or real estate brochure.

"Thank you for this," she said, her voice raised a bit to cover the few feet of distance she'd put between them. "Much better than the boring gym."

He was keeping track of her in his peripheral vision, but doing his best not to look directly at her after their near-collision. The fact that he found the mother of his child about as hot as they came didn't have any good place in his life. He wasn't an animal. He could overcome baser instincts.

But as her perfectly shaped, strong-looking thighs moved up and down with the pedals, he had to fight the temptation to think about those legs without the leggings and T-shirt covering them. Even her cute little brand-new silver glitter tennis shoes were a turn-on.

She'd pulled her hair back into a ponytail before she'd arrived that morning, and with the bike helmet on, she certainly wasn't ready for a model runway, and yet, the damn thing just seemed to make her sexier to him.

Tricia had worn the exact same helmet. He didn't remember it looking like that on her. But then, Gavin had always been on bike rides with them.

He'd let the boy take the bike he'd bought for him with him when he'd had to leave. And had been told that Gavin had traded it for a couple of joints the previous summer.

"You told me you ride most days after work," she said as they rounded a curve, and what could be seen of his house from the road came into view. The drive was circular and round, passing through trees to the house before going by a three-car garage and heading back out again.

"I do." He wondered if Talley knew he was out there. If she'd be wagging her tail thinking he'd be pulling in the drive. So far, his girl had been showing signs of improvement. He was hesitantly optimistic that they'd weathered the storm.

"Is it some kind of training?" she asked. "Do you ride in marathons?"

He shook his head. "My job challenges me all day long," he told her. "I ride at night to unwind, not to bring on more challenge."

"I get it," she said, and when he glanced over, she was smiling.

And he had the sudden urge to kiss her.

They'd ridden through the entire neighborhood. Amelia felt kind of disappointed as she recognized that they were approaching the corner where they'd started. She found it a little odd that she hadn't seen another soul outside during the entire ride, but with all the trees and the properties stretching behind the homes, she figured anyone who might be out that Sunday afternoon wouldn't be visible from the road.

"You good to go around again, or are you ready to get back?" Craig asked, slowing down as he rode close enough that they could have normal conversation.

"I'm fine to go again," she told him, glad that he'd offered her the chance to enjoy a bit more of the day's beauty, the exhilarating feeling of pure, healthy enjoyment. Though she had a lot of work waiting for her and, more importantly, designs she was excited to work on, she wasn't ready to be home alone for the rest of the evening.

She could always call Angie. Their friends in LA were a bit far for an impromptu Sunday evening rendezvous, but she and her sister could have dinner together. She knew her sister had been planning to spend the afternoon and evening getting caught up at the office.

Pulling her cell phone out from where she'd tucked it in the waistband of her pants, she dialed her sister and got her voicemail. Probably meant Angie was on an important call. Although Amelia was the one who would be getting any emergency contacts from the factory. And she wouldn't be on with accounts on a Sunday afternoon.

"You need to get back?" Craig asked, glancing at her phone.

"No." With one hand steering, she attempted to shove her phone back into the waistband that, as it turned out, had been much easier to pull from one-handed than push into. Feeling like an uncoordinated nut, she quickly shoved her hand beneath the neckline of her shirt and deposited the phone in the top of her sport bra.

And noticed the flower beds around the trees at the house they were passing. The birdbath on the lawn. Was it Craig's house?

She didn't see him as a flower bed kind of guy. But then, he probably had a landscaper who took care of his yard for him. The next house was more exposed than most—its yard almost bare, other than the massive fountain that was in the center of a circular drive. The house was blue.

Didn't seem like Craig, either. He wasn't an opulent, fountain-in-the-front-yard kind of guy.

Of course, Tricia could have been that kind of woman. The house had originally been hers.

He was living in a house that had been purchased by his ex-lover. The thought gave her a stumble. And she straightened up inside.

"Okay," she said as they turned a corner. "This is kind of stupid. I appreciate that you respect the fact that we aren't going to make this personal. And you're right, I wouldn't have accepted if you'd suggested I come to your home." She was riding too close to him as she spoke. Thought she caught a whiff of the slightly musky scent that had lingered in her home after he'd left the night before. "But there's no harm in you pointing out which is yours."

So she could quit obsessing over something so insignificant.

If he didn't want her to know, he shouldn't have brought her to his neighborhood. While it was the perfect Sunday ride, it wasn't the only quiet area in a city known to be a haven for some of Hollywood's elite. The fact that Marie Cove had very little public beach area, and was out in the middle of virtually nowhere, also helped to preserve its small-town aura.

"I'm happy to show you," Craig said. "We can stop in if you need to use the facilities or anything, get more water."

She'd sipped a few times, but still had half a bottle. "No, I'm good," she told him. There was no reason for her to see his home. Wasn't a good idea. Curiosity killed the cat.

Where that cliché had popped up from, she didn't know, but figured it apropos.

And because she wasn't in line for becoming a cat, dead or alive, she purposely didn't stare when, a few minutes later, Craig pointed to a storybook-looking place, white with black shutters, at least two stories, set within trees and far enough back from the road that you wouldn't hear traffic. "That's it," he said.

The lawn was a perfect green, freshly cut. "All of these places have the same circular drive," was all she said.

His house was perfect. If you were a person who believed what you read in storybooks. Who believed you got married and happily loved someone for the rest of your life.

"You don't like it," he said, coming closer as they rolled past his property.

"No, I do," she told him, glancing his way without quite as much trouble now that she saw where that great bod lived. "It's perfectly lovely."

"But?"

"But what?" It truly was a gorgeous place. As gorgeous as the man who'd bought it so that it would be available for the boy he'd raised to come home to it...whenever.

"I don't know, that's why I asked. Your expression... Is there something about the house you don't like?"

Okay, if they were going to know each other, even casually, he was going to have to quit reading her like that proverbial book.

They pedaled slowly. Amelia concentrated on the warmth of the sun on her cheeks, mingling with the cool breeze in the seventy-degree air.

"It's truly a beautiful place," she told him, meaning it. And if he was going to read her, he'd have to know that, too. "The lawn is immaculate. Like a Disney movie scene."

"Thank you, I work hard at it."

"You did it yourself?"

"I mowed it yesterday, before I came to your place."

Shirtless? She immediately rejected the first thought that occurred to her. And was left with the second, which was that she liked the idea that he mowed his own grass.

"You have a riding mower?" she asked. Duane had had one. And then had hired a kid to ride it twice a week.

"Yes, and a push one, too. It's easier around the trees."

She hadn't thought of the challenge presented by so many trees. Thought how much easier it would have been to just cut them down rather than mow around them every week.

And admired the guy who chose to keep them.

"So we're agreed the yard is lovely," he said teasingly, and then more seriously, "but what don't you like?"

"From what I could see, which wasn't much, I liked it all." She had. And then added, "For someone else."

She paused and then continued.

"I don't believe in storybooks." Didn't matter if he knew. If he liked her or not. The only thing that mattered was him being satisfied that she was going to be a good parent for his child.

"Homes like that…they give me the heebies. So many times, the stories that go on inside them aren't at all how they appear from the outside."

"Let me guess, you grew up in a home like that."

She nodded. "Yep," she told him, and pedaled hard enough to pull in front of him.

"Maybe if you were inside my house, you'd see that healthy love can live there." Craig didn't know why he'd caught up to her when she so clearly needed a moment. Why he was pushing when she was giving him so much more than she had to give.

Amelia shook her head, but didn't look his way. "You think I haven't been inside a lovely home without a sad tale inside?" she asked him, and he realized he'd short-changed her with his latest assumptions. "I've got a couple of high school friends who grew up in my neighborhood who now have their own fairy-tale homes," she told him. "I love visiting them. I love their houses. I just don't ever, ever want to live in one."

He thought of her condominium—which easily matched the square footage of his home—and felt like he wanted to change her mind. Knew that he had no business even entertaining the thought.

"I'm great visiting my friends' homes," she said. "I'm even fine visiting the home I grew up in. My mom and Duane are still there. But the thought of living in one of them…it makes my chest tight. Like I'm chained down." She gave a huff. "For someone who needs you to know that I'm fine parenting material, I'm suddenly sounding slightly neurotic," she added, but didn't stop pedaling just as fast.

"I didn't have a fairy-tale childhood," she told him. "You already know that. I've risen above my past. I've taken control of my destiny, rather than blaming others for my pain, but you don't come from bad without any scars."

He'd circled them back around to the exit, cutting off the back half of the neighborhood, and she slowed to a stop as they came to the small gate. Swipe card in hand, Craig looked over at her and found her gaze locked on him. Completely openeyed, looking him straight in the eye.

"I've got issues," she told him. "I'm aware of them. And I tend to them. My home doesn't have a yard. Or an attached garage. And it's not the only one in the building. But it's as large, as quiet and, to me, as beautiful as any home on this street. I feel safe there. Secure. And I feel life around me, too. Other people, with other stories, facing other challenges, all of us getting through it all separately, but together, too. I need that. Other people, strangers, living their lives in and around mine."

Her honesty struck him hard. In a deep way.

Good and bad ways. In some ways he felt so connected to her, oddly, almost ethereally—in part, he knew, because she was carrying his child. But in other ways, she was the antithesis of everything he wanted.

A woman having his child who was not his wife.

A woman who never intended to marry. A woman he admired more than he'd ever thought possible.

Who turned him on in ways no other woman ever had. Turned him on because she was looking at him from beneath a bike helmet and still exuded a strength that spoke to him.

"Fair enough," he told her. "But I was thinking..." He let them through the small gate and started slowly toward their cars. "How about if we make this our thing, three times a week—the bike riding? We'll just meet up—you get the exercise you need without dying of boredom, and I get to reassure myself that everything is going well with your child. It'll be my way of checking in, and to find out if the baby needs anything that I can help with."

"I could just agree to call you if the baby needs anything."

"You could." He slowed his pedaling as their

cars drew close. "Or you could ride with me, enjoy the exercise and have something to tell your child about me when she grows up and has questions about her 'Y' component."

They were both using "her" more often now. Was that somehow a sign that she was having a girl? A daughter?

Biologically, *his* daughter?

He was a doctor. A man of science. Was this thought-stream a sign that he was losing his mind?

"Can we try this another time or two before I commit to three times a week?"

The air was crisp and sweet as he pulled in a healthy dose, feeding his lungs. "Sure," he told her. "And if it helps you make up your mind, it won't be forever. I wouldn't recommend riding at all during your third trimester."

He'd already told her that. The night before.

And warned himself that if he didn't watch himself he *could* lose his mind.

Over her.

Chapter Twelve

They rode every Tuesday, Thursday and Sunday for the next six weeks. Sometimes their journeys were mostly silent, consisting of brief hellos and then the quiet they both craved after long days at work. Sometimes, usually on Sundays, they talked a bit more—generic conversations that left her frustrated sometimes, but mostly peaceful, too.

And other than those rides, they never communicated at all. No phone calls. No texts. Each time they rode, they determined the location and time of the next meet, and they met.

She was even getting used to the effect his body

in riding gear had on her. Figured that eventually it wouldn't faze her anymore.

When her pregnancy hormones settled down. That's all it was. The hormones. Craig Harmon was no different than any other man. He just was the only one in her close proximity and so perfectly handsome, while her hormones were raging.

Every time they met, at different spots depending on where they were riding, Craig asked how she was feeling, his gaze landing on her stomach.

And always, she wore a baggy T-shirt so he couldn't see the way her belly was starting to fill with a baby. The child was hers. Not his. She needed to keep that designation firmly protected.

She'd had her sixteen-week ultrasound. He'd known when it was, but hadn't asked how it went. Just posed his usual, general query about how she was feeling and stopped there. She'd said, as she always did, that she was just fine.

Angie had been with her for the ultrasound. They'd heard a healthy, strong heartbeat. Had cried a little. She didn't want to know the sex. Not then.

But as her body continued to fill out, as more and more evidence that her son or daughter was really growing inside her—her child, her family— she grew more and more curious. Now that the baby was viable, not just test tubes and doctors and biology...

Angie thought she should find out so she could start buying clothes and things for the nursery. And yet, she hesitated, and she couldn't figure out why.

Craig had talked to her about the sex of the baby that very first day they'd met. He'd seemed to want to know, too. It was a valid response. She understood that.

But every time she picked up the phone to call the Parent Portal, to have someone look at her chart and tell her, she got butterflies in her stomach and turned her thoughts back to work. It began to weigh on her—this indecision—because she didn't understand it.

She talked to Angie about it one day as they sat over lunch celebrating a newly signed contract with the lace maker in the south of France. Her sister thought maybe she was hoping for one sex over the other and was afraid of feeling disappointed.

It made sense—especially for Amelia, who couldn't stand to, in any way, not be perfect for those she loved. And yet, Angie's theory didn't ring true.

Imagining a life raising a son was equally as heady as imagining a life with a daughter; each was different in some ways, and gloriously the same in others. They both brought exciting and wonderful possibilities.

She put the fear of calling the clinic down to pregnancy hormones any time it overwhelmed her. Those were a great catchall. And a legitimate possible culprit.

They were the reason she was beginning to look forward to her rides with Craig so much. Why those rides were becoming the highlight of her weeks. Because of hormones.

She'd read that a side effect of pregnancy could be a woman craving sex more, figured that having that particular malady was better than having morning sickness, which had left her completely alone thus far.

And just like morning sickness did for other women, she knew her raging sex drive would soon disappear.

The last Sunday in February marked the sixth week of bike riding. They'd been taking longer, though still moderately paced, routes and that Sunday had predetermined to meet at an entrance to the private beach that Amelia's condo had access to. From there they were biking along an ocean-view walkway that meandered for several miles, having been converted years before from a rail-road track.

Craig had been getting more and more nervous about her biking on roads with vehicles, which had been his main reason for vetoing her suggestion that they ride along the cliff at the edge of town. She'd pointed out that if it wasn't safe for her, it wasn't safe for him, either, but the comment had kind of slithered off to the ether, where it most likely belonged.

His comment to her, while seeming personal, had, in actuality, been in line with their agreement. He'd been looking to the safety and well-being of the baby she carried. While her comment…it could only have been an expression of her concern for him.

Of course, human beings commonly expressed compassion or concern for perfect strangers. It was one of the beauties of being human—the oneness of the experience and the bonding of souls simply because they were of like species.

As always, she'd worn leggings and an oversized T-shirt for the ride, strapping her water bottle beneath her top and below her bump, which was becoming noticeable. She might not look pregnant yet to a stranger on the street, but to anyone who knew her, she'd definitely put on girth. Her weight gain, while a little below average for a woman at twenty weeks of pregnancy, was still within the acceptable range.

Craig had the bikes down and waiting by the time she approached. The sight of him in his usual bike shorts and a black spandex, short-sleeved top made her normal brain malfunction and she was suddenly seeing a vision of him standing there without clothes. Inviting her to do with him what she liked.

Oh, Lord, she liked…it all. Everything. His hands. His lips. His tongue. *Him.*

At least, in the vision that she quickly shoved away she did. In her mind and heart…she knew better.

It was hormones.

"You feeling okay?" His concerned expression got her all riled up again. Having this…this…man care…she kind of melted a little.

"Of course," she told him. And wondered what he'd do if she blurted out that she was feeling flashes of desire over him. "I feel great."

But not as great as his smile looked, or felt down to her core, when he poured it on her. It had only been two days since she'd seen the man— not months. She could not possibly be starved for the sight of him.

It was just the hormones.

* * *

She was wearing another damn, oversized T-shirt. Craig was starving for the sight of Amelia Grace carrying his child and he got a flowing T-shirt. How many of those things did she own?

Still, it gave him another dose of those femininely muscular and long legs. From there he allowed himself a quick glance at her face, which was expressive and intriguing because you never knew what it was going to show you next. And those eyes changed colors—from green to gold—based on what she was feeling, not necessarily what she was saying.

She wasn't fine. Had looked away when he smiled at her, and her hand had jerked when he'd touched it with the bike handle. Something was bothering her.

And it wasn't his to own. Or even borrow long enough to see if he could fix it.

So he got on his bike. Waited for her to mount hers. And started off down the paved path that was wide enough for two-way traffic, and for them to ride side by side. She started out behind him, anyway, and he was concentrating on the things that were in his circle of control. The use of the most expedient muscles for pedaling, the straightness of his back and the strength of his grip on the handlebars. He took in the ocean off to the distance on his right. Some of the people who were on the path with them. A couple of joggers. Three in-line skaters passing in the other direction.

Clouds blocked the sun that Sunday afternoon, making the seventy-three-degree temperature seem chillier, and laying a gray shadow over their surroundings, but he took in a breath of air that felt...alive. More alive than he'd been in a long time.

He slowed his pace a bit, meaning she'd either do so, as well, to stay behind him, or ride up to join him. Choice was hers.

"How's Talley doing?" she asked as she joined him.

"Great." He gave her a quick smile so she'd know she was welcome beside him. That the conversation was welcome. Thursday's ride had been through city neighborhoods and they'd passed the vet. He'd told her all about his dog, that Talley had an appointment there the next day to have her numbers run again, one more time, just to see where they were at. "Everything's within normal range." Sugars, most importantly—that meant the pancreas was doing its job again.

"Oh, thank goodness." The emotion in her tone

was startling. She'd been worried about his dog? Was she an animal lover, then?

"Does your condo association allow pets?" he asked her. He hadn't noticed a pet park or dog-walking area when he'd been there.

"Yes," she told him. "That was a must for me."

"You have one?" Perhaps a cat who'd deigned him not worthy of her appearance the one time he'd been inside her place.

"Not right now. But I don't want to live someplace where I can't ever have one."

The woman was just so fascinating to him. Contradictory, and yet...not really. Either she just plain couldn't make decisions and so had to plan for every eventuality, or she knew herself well enough to plan for the possible eventualities.

"You like pets, then."

"Yeah. But I was thinking about my baby, too. What if he wants a dog someday? I want to live in a home that can accommodate that."

He. For a long time, she'd been using *she* most often. Did that mean she knew the sex of the child? She'd had the ultrasound weeks ago. He'd wanted to ask, but thought it best to let her share as she saw fit any information that was nonessential to health and security.

But...*he*. There'd be a boy in the world who

was a part of him. Who might look like him. Have the same birthmark on his shoulder. The same ear shape. The same thick beard that required twice daily shaving if he wanted to go without shadow…

He did a mental retake, brought himself back to the topic at hand. Pets. Innocuous as always.

"Did you have a pet growing up?" he asked.

"Tiki," she said, barely missing a breath as they pedaled. "She was a Poochin—a cross between a poodle and a Japanese Chin. We got her for Christmas when Angie was two and I was three. I think, with Angie getting so independent, Mom wanted another baby in the house."

She was smiling, which made him smile. Angie came up a lot in Amelia's conversation. He'd asked to meet the other woman, but Amelia had never responded to his request. And, of course, he couldn't push.

"How long did you have her?" he asked, eager for another peek into her private world.

"Until my junior year of high school. But we almost lost her once, which is why I could relate to what you were going through with Talley."

Two bikes were coming from the opposite direction and Craig sped up to allow Amelia to fall in behind him and be more safely out of the way. When she rejoined him, he asked, "What happened to Tiki to make you almost lose her?" It was like he couldn't stop himself from soaking in whatever she'd offer up. He had to know everything he could know about this beautiful woman. For his peace of mind where the baby was concerned, yes, but he could no longer deny that there was more to it than that. That his interest was more personal.

"The vet thought she had cancer."

He'd been expecting a near–car accident. Or a runaway incident. Maybe a dangerous bug bite.

"He said we needed to do a biopsy, which would cost about six hundred dollars. Duane said spending that kind of money on a ten-year-old dog was wasteful and said we couldn't have the test done."

"But your mom had the test done, anyway," he surmised when she didn't finish her story. "Did the vet agree to take payments in installments?"

"Nope. Duane said no and Mom always did what Duane said."

Ah. The lightning bolt hit him late. Based on what she'd told him about her mother, about herself, in relationships, he should certainly have seen that one coming.

They pedaled silently for a block or two. Slowing their pace. Most of the time they had the sidewalk to themselves—due mostly to the cloudy sky, he figured.

"So what happened with your dog?" he asked when he couldn't find a way to just let it go.

"Duane told Mom we should have her put to sleep."

Anger flared in his gut, and harsh words stopped just short of flying out his mouth as she continued.

"Angie and I stayed up most of that night. Crying. Holding her. And the next morning we went with Mom to the vet. I asked him if there was some way to do the test and let Angie and I work off the payment. We'd already agreed we'd clean poop out of cages if we had to, or spend Saturdays washing floors..."

Her smile was more quirky than sad. And again he was filled with admiration. And something more. An understanding, maybe. Amelia Grace was not a woman who said things she didn't mean. She thought things through. She looked for her answers. And she implemented them. The baby she was carrying was proof of that.

"An older woman in the waiting room overheard me and offered to pay for the biopsy," Amelia was saying. "Turned out she lived not far from us, had a lot of money and was all alone. Angie and I visited her after school a few times a month at least for the next few years, until she moved to be closer to her son. She had the most amazing stories to tell…"

"And Tiki?" he asked, grateful for that name-less older woman. Gratified at the validation that many good and decent people lived in the world.

"She didn't have cancer. She just had a clogged duct." Amelia's words brought relief, even though he'd calculated the dog had lived another three years.

"And how did you explain to Duane that the dog hadn't been put to sleep?"

"We told him the truth. At which time he'd told my mom that he was glad they hadn't wasted the money on a test that proved unnecessary to begin with. But to be fair, he was drunk all three nights this was going on."

There was no bitterness in her tone. And he figured he knew why. While Amelia had been unable to control much of what happened to and around her while she'd been growing up, she'd taken control of her life, pieces at a time, as she'd been able. Like finding a way to save her dog. And in doing so, by finding her own powers, she'd found acceptance for what had been.

If he were to be completely honest with himself, he didn't really need to see her anymore to have peace of mind where his child was concerned. That baby might not live in a traditional home, might not live in the type of home Craig wanted for him and his family, but he or she was going to have one helluva fantastic mother.

Chapter Thirteen

Amelia really enjoyed the ride that Sunday afternoon. Even more than usual. Talking to Craig was like talking to her counselor sometimes—she could say things without worrying. Her words weren't going to hurt his feelings. Their opinions didn't need to coincide with the other's desires.

His combination of knowledge and experience gave him good insights.

And he was a good listener.

And yet, she wasn't paying him to listen to her. Nor was he bound under any kind of laws or certification to withhold his own opinion, or to draw out hers.

They just *talked*.

And he listened because he chose to do so, not because it was his job. Just as she did when he talked about Talley and the other things going on in his life—like his mom and dad's thirty-fifth anniversary coming up that summer. He wanted to make it special for them but wasn't able to land on what to do. Or the partner who was leaving his clinic to make more money in Los Angeles. They'd had a good talk about the value of money, how much was enough, a few Sundays before. They both wanted enough financial security to be able to do the things they wanted to do, but neither of them felt the need to live more lavishly than their current circumstances. He hoped to have a small yacht someday. Something big enough to spend the night out on the ocean. She wanted to be able to take her child on meaningful and exciting trips around the world. And to have season passes to Disneyland.

He wanted a house full of kids and she couldn't help thinking what a great dad he would make. She wanted just the one child she was having, or at the most two. She had a business to run and didn't want to stretch herself so thin that she had to miss functions, not be available to help with homework or to just be present and sit and listen to her child regurgitate everything that had happened in her day.

She didn't want to miss any of the chatter.

And as they fell silent and the conversation started to replay through her mind, she couldn't deny the pang of sadness she felt at the realization that her own child wouldn't get the benefit of having any dad, let alone Craig.

As they pulled to a stop at a little shack with restrooms, a vending machine and a couple of benches inside, she noticed that there wasn't anyone else around. They were often by themselves when they rode, but because they were on the paved exercise path, and because there'd been others out skating and jogging and riding with them, she was surprised to have the bathroom completely to herself. The bathroom need that was becoming more prevalent these days. She did her business and came out to find Craig standing under the roof of the open portion of the shack.

Walled in on three sides, the open portion faced the trail and behind that the ocean in the far distance with acres of natural parkland with some trees in between them and the shore of huge boulders a few feet below.

"Didn't you say you'd read there was zero chance of rain today?" Craig asked as she came back out into the little vestibule with the benches and vending machine.

"Yeah," she told him, glancing out at the nearly dark sky.

"I did, too."

Apparently the weather report had been wrong. And she'd been too busy enjoying her time with him to pay attention to a path that had been slowly emptying of people.

"You think we can make it back without getting wet?" She wasn't worried. Wasn't really even bothered. Sitting alone with him in the little shack through a downpour didn't sound dreadful. She had a vision of a cabin in the wilderness, all-day rain, and her and Craig, cozy inside, and pushed it quickly away. She had to stop seeing castles in the clouds.

Craig had pulled out his phone, was asking his virtual assistant for a weather report.

The report came back that there was a twenty percent chance of rain. Amelia followed him outside. Turned a circle, still looking up at the sky.

"It's completely blue over there," she said, pointing inland. Another biker, heading back toward town, slowed down, mentioned the darkness coming in over the ocean. The three of them discussed heading back or waiting it out, just in case.

The other biker, a man about their age, was going for it, finishing his ride. Amelia figured they could, too.

Craig had the exact opposite idea. "The track will be more slippery," he said. "I don't want to take any chances on you falling."

She wasn't going to fall. His concern was overkill. And nice. Beyond nice.

She could easily become addicted to the attention he gave her.

But it was getting darker. The path really could get slick. And so she let herself stay alone in the shack with him, waiting out the rain.

Craig felt better about waiting out the storm, figured it was the right choice for the baby's sake, just until the dark clouds dissipated, and yet, he knew it would have been much better for them had they left. Or for him. Sitting there, in a tiny little three-walled shack, seemingly alone in the world with Amelia Grace, felt…intimate. Personal.

"I have a question I've been wanting to ask you, but don't want to open any doors," she said as the silence settled around them on their bench for two, which was just a few painted two-by-fours nailed to four wooden legs. She settled against the wall behind them and as she leaned back her T-shirt settled around the small bulge in her belly.

That little lump hit him hard enough to knock the air out of him. Just as she was wanting to keep doors closed.

He wanted to reassure her that he would comply with her request, but couldn't speak for a second so he nodded. He'd do whatever she needed. He knew that.

Didn't mean it would be easy.

Or pleasant.

"Why did you want to know the sex of the baby?"

Hmmph. She was killing him. Slowly. Because he'd begged her to let him be a presence in her life. He was right where he wanted to be.

"Honestly?" The words came because the question had an answer. And because he wouldn't let himself wonder why she was asking it. "So that when I'm in town, years from now, and see a boy that reminds me of my father, or pictures I've seen of myself, I won't wonder if he's mine if I know the child is a girl. Or vice versa, if I see a girl that looks like pictures I've seen of my mother…"

Turning her head along the wall, she glanced at him right as he was looking at her. Their gazes locked as she studied him and he wished he knew what she was thinking. Wished it hard.

"I know I'm going to wonder," he added softly. "At least if I know the sex of the child, I'll only wonder for the half the population."

There. The whole truth. She'd asked.

And looked away at that last response.

He had no know idea what she'd been seeking.

"I'm afraid to know." A new tone had entered her voice. Was it uncertainty?

"Why?" He was truly curious.

Her shrug, and glance in his direction, made him want to take her in his arms and hold her tenderly. For as long as either of them needed the contact.

"I can't figure it out," she told him. "Angie thinks it's because I'm afraid I'll be disappointed. You know, if I really want a boy and it's a girl. Or vice versa." She kind of mocked the way he'd said that same thing a moment before, and accompanied the words with a self-deprecating grin and a shake of her head.

"I know it's not that. I will be happy either way. I ask myself what I truly want, deep down, and all I ever come up with is a healthy baby. So I think I'm, you know, parroting in my brain what I know should be the best answer, but I just keep coming back to it. I really just want a healthy baby."

She leaned her head against the wall again, staring slightly upward.

He couldn't help another long glance at that small protrusion of her T-shirt. Was it sick for a guy to get turned on by the sight of a woman carrying his child?

He'd never seen Tricia pregnant. Hadn't known Gavin as a newborn.

He'd loved him as though he'd been his own, though, but nothing about his previous life had prepared him for the current one.

Nothing in his medical background told him it was wrong to find his personal involvement with pregnancy sexy. To the contrary. If a patient had come to him, asking the same question, he'd have said he thought it was probably natural.

"My whole life, as long as I can remember, this is what I've wanted most," she told him. "A baby of my own. A child to raise, innocent laughter in my home. Questions. Exploring the world through eyes that don't know it all yet. Watching the way the freedom to challenge what you don't understand plays itself out. Even the certainty and know-it-all-ness of the teen years. And the middle-of-the-night feedings. I can't wait for those nights when I'm so tired and have to pull myself out of bed, anyway. Because that's love. Real love."

Craig suddenly knew, there in a shack that was getting chilly as they sat there in their sweat-dampened riding clothes, that exact moment was when he fell in love with the mother of his child.

Craig's silence made Amelia uncomfortable. She'd said too much. Got too comfortable with him. She'd actually forgotten for a few minutes that, per the boundaries they set, per all agreements, he could only be the biological donor to the dream she'd been sharing with him.

She'd really just wanted to know why he'd wanted to know the sex of their child. And she was trying to understand the fight going on inside her and wasn't ready to seek counseling about it yet. Didn't really think it warranted that. It was just bugging the hell out of her. She'd look at the phone, think about calling to find out the baby's sex, get all tense then feel relieved when she let herself off the hook.

"So how does knowing the sex of the baby in your lifelong plan change anything?" Craig asked, as though finishing her thought.

She thought about the question. It was one she hadn't asked herself. One Angie hadn't even touched on. Maybe because it was irrelevant. How *did* knowing the sex change things?

It didn't really. Just... "It makes it more real," she said. Which was a great thing—having her dreams coming to life. So that wouldn't be the cause of the tension. Would it?

As tension started to seep into her, she looked over at him, needing to know he was real, too. That he was there as a donor, but also as her friend.

Needing to know how he seemed to know her so well. Or at least read her well.

"I'm afraid to believe it's going to happen."

"Why?"

"Because if I believe and then something goes wrong..."

She was scared to death to believe she was really going to have a family of her own. To believe that healthy love would live in her home.

Because she was scared to death she couldn't ever have that—a healthy, loving home. That such things were for other people. Not her.

Their faces were so close, their mouths both open, as though either of them was ready to speak. Amelia had no thought, no plan, no warning before she leaned just enough to close that distance. Her lips touched his lightly. Tentatively. For a brief second he made it more than that, filling her body with an ache it had never known, and she jerked back.

"The baby's not viable yet," she blurted loudly what she'd only been acknowledging to herself. Needing to pretend that she hadn't just done what she had. Needing him to let it go, as though it hadn't happened. They didn't need this…couldn't chance ruining what they were building for the baby by letting sexual attraction get involved. "I don't want to believe…" She had to stop to catch her breath, to focus on what she was saying and not on him. "To name him, to fall in love, until I know the baby is viable." That was it. And it made perfect sense.

At least something did.

"You think you haven't already fallen in love?"

He wasn't smiling, but his expression was kind as he looked at her, and then at the hands she'd unconsciously placed on her stomach. He was letting her off the hook. Letting the kiss go.

Amelia sat up as a surprising spurt of tears sprang to her eyes.

Hormones. It was just hormones.

Or he was right. She'd fallen in love with her baby before she'd said she could, in spite of herself—and maybe fallen a little bit in love with her baby's father, too.

Chapter Fourteen

Craig knew something was wrong the second he saw Amelia's face on Tuesday of that week. There was nothing overt, no frown or worry lines. She smiled, greeted him as usual, went immediately to the bike he had standing in the parking lot waiting for her. It was a lack of something that caught his attention. She seemed slightly vacant. Like she was wearing a facade to complete her day.

He had had a hectic day with four patients calling in for emergency appointments, in addition to an already full schedule. He'd had to order extra blood work for a man not much older than himself, a man who was married and had two little ones at home. He was hoping that the test was merely going to show them that nothing was wrong, but his gut was telling him differently. That young family might not have a lifetime together. It was one of the moments he wished he was anything but a doctor.

And that day it carried another weight attached to it. He was feeling for a father who might not be around for his kids and for kids who might not get to have their father around…and in a sense, that was his own fate. And the fate of his child.

They were riding in the neighborhood closest to Amelia's condominium, as both of them had been pressed for time and had planned only a forty-five-minute spin. They'd made that decision on Sunday as they'd returned from their short stay at the facility shack. The dark clouds had dispersed within fifteen minutes and no rain had fallen—as predicted.

Amelia had been different on the ride back, too, he reminded himself. Something he'd pondered probably more than necessary in the time since.

All to no good resolution. She had such walls around her, and as much as he felt compelled to penetrate those walls, to care and be there for her and show her that the world offered unending possibility for happiness, he knew that his place in her life required that he not penetrate anything where she was concerned.

The knowing didn't stop him caring, unfortunately. Which wasn't keeping him in the best of moods, either.

And yet, there he was, ready to trek around a neighborhood with her, eager to, rather than getting in the more rigorous coastal ride his day called for. He seemed to be some kind of masochist where this woman was concerned.

Because he cared. No going back on that one. He'd acknowledged it. He had feelings for her. They were there.

"You ready?" She took off before he did, leaving him to follow her. It had happened before. They took turns leading the way. So why did it bother him that afternoon?

When they rode for twenty minutes in silence, he told himself that was a good thing. The way it should be. Going according to plan. The vagaries of his day started to fade, and he noticed that the sky was a perfect blue with the sun setting over the trees in what would be a fantastic picture for someone into the art of photography.

He was into his work. His home and Talley. His parents. Friends from college. Bike riding, a good game of tennis. Racquetball. Sun and sand and time at the ocean. An occasional, lazy day binge watching television.

And Amelia Grace. He'd ridden up beside her a few times. In front of her twice. And behind her for the majority of the ride. She'd yielded to cars and pedestrians in the moderately busy neighborhood, swerving to miss a ball that bounced from a couple of boys in a yard to the street in front of them.

He'd reprimanded himself for trying to get another glimpse of the small bump he'd seen two days before during their little shack retreat.

And wondered if she'd felt the baby kick yet. Once she felt that intimate proof of life, she'd either relax and let herself believe her dreams were coming true. Or she'd panic more, fearing that she was going to get that close to happiness and then lose again. Either way, he wanted to be aware when it was happening.

As they turned to head back, signaling the last half of the ride—really the last quarter, as their turning point was closer to their cars than the distance they'd traveled from them—he pedaled up next to her.

"You mad at me?" he asked. Those moments while they'd waited out the dark clouds on Sunday might have changed things for her, too. Not that they'd talk about that. But if he'd somehow revealed more of what he'd been feeling than he'd thought, or intended, it was up to him to reassure her that nothing was changing between them. His feelings…they were *his*. He'd deal with them on his own. Separate and apart from her and their agreement.

"Of course not." She glanced at him, frowning. "Why you would think that? What could I have to be angry with you about? Unless…" She slowed her bike. "Did you do something I don't know about that's going to piss me off?"

Like fall in love with her? Even just temporarily? God, let it be temporary.

"You've just been off today. Something's bothering you." He didn't ask. He wasn't giving her the chance to deny her mood. To make her feel as though she had to lie to him.

"I'm just…pondering," she said. She'd kept the slower pace and he adjusted his speed to match hers, riding closer to her so that they could talk.

"Anything you want to talk about?"

She glanced at him, a strand of long auburn hair, having escaped from her helmet, touching her cheek and shoulder and dangling down her arm. She never wore jewelry when they rode, but he'd noticed a while back that she had pierced ears. Had thought of buying her a pair of garnet earrings once when he'd seen them displayed at the mall, figuring they'd bring out the highlights in her hair.

That had been before he'd known he was in trouble. Before he'd realized he was falling for her. But he should have known. When he'd seen the earrings, he'd been at the mall with Kim, one of the two women he'd had semiserious relationships with since Tricia's death. They'd run into each other one afternoon at the grocery store—which was where they'd first met. Thinking that now he was finding his peace of mind regarding his donated sperm, he might be more able to get on with finding a woman to settle down with, he had asked her out. They'd gone out the past few Friday nights.

But not the next one. Not now that he knew that he was harboring temporary feelings for the woman carrying his child.

Amelia hadn't answered him about whether she had something on her mind. Apparently she didn't want to talk about it. Whatever it was.

Not him. That's all that should concern him, all that was within his circle of control. Unless something was bothering her that he could help with. Something other than not understanding her fear of finding out the sex of her child. Something new.

Had she found out the sex of the baby since they

had last spoken? He glanced toward the T-shirt bagging out over her thighs as she pedaled. Was it a girl? A boy? Would he have a son in the world who'd learn to throw a baseball without him? A little girl who didn't have a daddy to take her to a father-daughter dance? If they even did those anymore.

"There's this New York designer..." Amelia's words broke into his thoughts so abruptly it took him a second to get up to speed with her. Apparently she did "want to talk about it."

"He asked Angie to come work for him. She would be designing exclusively rather than part-time, the way things are now, where she has to spend so much time helping to run the business."

His gut sank. This wasn't little. Amelia's family was everything to her. Angie was all set up to be a prominent security source for Amelia's child. He was surprised she was even riding at all. And so calmly.

"Does she want to go?"

"No. And she told him so. She told me she loves being the boss, and I know that she does," she said, glancing at him. "She's always been a little bossy."

"And you aren't?" The teasing words came out of him naturally, as though they were friends.

She grinned, as he'd meant her to do, and said,

"Of course I am. Which is why we share that position at Feel Good." She sobered then; he saw her expression flatten out, as if she was not even aware of what houses they were passing. In that moment, she was everything to him.

"She doesn't want to go, and yet you're still bothered. Does that mean you think she should?"

"I don't know what I think, and that's why I'm bothered."

He was beginning to see a pattern. Amelia didn't get upset about problems or having to fix them. She got upset when she didn't know *how* to fix them.

He could relate to that. One hundred percent.

"I think the position would be fun for her. And it's certainly a compliment that she was even asked. But I don't know that she'd be happy in New York. And I'm pretty certain she wouldn't be happy living that far from home. And that's not really what's bugging me," she said. "I just… I have ideas for Feel Good, solid, researched and analyzed business choices for growth. Angie doesn't like them. She wants us to stay a smallish, family-owned business. So now that she's got this offer… I'm finding myself wanting to give her what she wants so she'll stay. And that's me being me. Trying to please, giving up what I think is best, for the one I love. Maybe I'm obsessing over her, trying too hard to compensate…

"Or am I? Growing Feel Good isn't like a driving need of mine. It's just sound business. But we're already comfortable enough. Anyway…the designer called this afternoon, sweetening his deal to Angie. He really wants her."

"How old is this guy?" An instant protective feeling sprang naturally to mind. He'd never met Amelia's sister, but if she looked anything like Amelia, she must be drop-dead gorgeous.

"Sixty-two. And he's gay," Amelia said, giving him a look and cocking her head at him. "Get your head out of the gutter, Harmon," she said. "Angie's just really that good."

He hadn't doubted Angie's talent for a second. Or her rightness for the job. He just…lived in a world where he now cared about both Grace sisters. Even the one he hadn't met. They were going to be raising his child together.

"Is she considering taking him up on his offer?"

"No. I just don't know if it's my job to encourage her to do so. I don't want her to go, but what if it's best for her?"

"I'd think that would be something she has to decide, right? As long as you aren't stopping her from going, or making it difficult to say she wants to go, then you've done your job."

She pulled to a halt at a stop sign they'd blown through two other times. There was no traffic on the quiet road now, either.

"How do you always know just what to say to me?" she asked.

He shrugged. Grinned. Made a joke to hide the truth.

He had a feeling he knew what to say because, for some truly god-awful reason, she was the woman with whom his soul currently wanted to connect.

Craig hadn't said anything more about the sex of the baby the rest of their ride. Amelia still felt uncomfortable for not having called the clinic. She'd figured, after Sunday's conversation, Craig would hold her accountable to facing her fears.

Instead, he'd picked up on her confusion over Angie's situation, and by the end of the ride she'd been more at ease where her younger sister was concerned. She'd done what she could, would continue to do it, to support her sister whichever way she chose, to love her and let her know life would be okay either way, and then she let it go.

What a concept! A relief. To do what she could and let the rest go.

It wasn't a new theory, of course.

She and her sister had dinner together at Amelia's condo Wednesday night and talked for hours. Wonderful hours. About growing up and hopes and dreams, about family and wants and needs. All stuff they'd been over before and delved into again as they talked about the future. No choices were made. Nothing changed between them. Probably not even the conversation, but for Amelia, it seemed new. And felt so good.

Increasingly at peace with the Angie situation, Amelia found herself almost obsessing about the sex of her baby on Thursday. While she waited for tea to brew she thought of boy names. And when she took a bathroom break, she had girl names on the brain. She still hadn't really felt the baby move. Not for sure. There'd been some bubbles that could have been movement.

She wasn't calling them that. Not until she knew for sure.

Now that they'd signed the deal for the "lace embellished jewelry," she had serious designing to do and had set aside hours on Thursday specifically for that purpose. Angie was handling all business calls, situations and problems for her as she sat holed up in her office, refusing to leave her drawing table, having to replace the lightbulb that illuminated the white top from underneath, and stay there until she'd produced something that pleased her.

She had sketched one earring. So similar to the prototype that she ripped off the page and threw it away. Picking up her tablet, she played with the electronic designing choices, and exited out of the program without saving. She picked up her pencil again, went back to the light board and drew a tiny denim jumper with lacy pockets and a colorful lacy butterfly sewn to the bib.

Baby clothes! Why hadn't she thought of that? Shaking her head, she ran for Angie, who was in her office next door on the phone. Judging by her frown, and the way her sister's mouth remained firm, she was on a business call that couldn't wait.

A new idea could.

She'd drawn a jumper instead of a bracelet. Did that mean she wanted a girl? *Was* having a girl? Or had the baby apparel been for a girl because... their customers, their product, was female based? A sudden vision of Craig holding a little girl in a lace embellished jumper had her drop her marker and turn off the board.

Back in her own office, knowing her sister

would seek her out once she'd taken care of whatever she was dealing with, Amelia thought again of Craig. He thought she was afraid to know the sex of the baby because she was afraid to let it be real until it was viable. Or had he just led her to figuring that out for herself?

Either way...there was truth in it. She was afraid to believe that she was really going to have her family. Afraid to let herself believe. To count on it.

Afraid to let herself try to open the door to more with the man who was taking up so many of her thoughts—and bringing such pleasure into her days? Afraid to acknowledge that she cared about him.

Afraid because she'd done all she could do, was doing all she could do, and the rest...was out of her control.

So...just like with Angie's decision, she had to let the fear go.

A vision of Craig came to mind, standing in his oh-so-sexy riding gear in between their bikes, waiting for her. As he would be in just a few hours. And the vision changed. One of the bikes had a stroller attached to the back with a sleeping bundle inside.

She had to call. To find out the sex of the baby. She'd tell him tonight.

He wanted to know. Telling him would be good for both of them. He seemed like her unofficial sponsor as she got over her need to hang on so tight to things that were out of her control.

That was it. She was going to call now. But as she glanced at her cell, she picked up her pencil, starting to draw. Fine metal chain links appeared, every two connected by a small lace rose. Beads appeared in bell caps, in place of the chain link… different stones for the various colors of lace she already knew she'd be getting.

The afternoon wore on. Angie came in, said they'd had to fire a packaging employee for anger-related issues, but that in the end, according to their plant manager, the woman had gone peace-fully. Angie was truly excited about the idea of ex-perimenting with baby clothes, was going to run to a box store, get some inexpensive items and start playing around with them.

And Amelia was already on her way to her meet with Craig—something Angie tolerated but still worried about—before she actually gave the voice command for her car system to dial the Parent Portal. She might not even be able to get ahold of someone who had the authority to look at her re-cords, her test results and give her the information she sought on such a short notice.

She'd promised herself she'd know by the time she saw Craig. That she'd tell him.

His body. Those riding pants. Images flashed. Confusing her as the ringing on the line played through her system. She was nervous, getting more tense with each ring. And she was growing moist down below, too.

He wasn't going to be a father to her baby, but she wanted him—it wasn't just hormones. The craving was growing worse, not easing off.

"The Parent Portal." The professional feminine voice cleared Amelia's mind.

"This is Amelia Grace. I had the NIPT several weeks ago and opted not to know the sex of my child, but I've changed my mind. Is there someone there who can get that information for me?"

If she'd chosen to use her own obstetrician, she could have called an office, but she hadn't. She'd wanted to stay at the Parent Portal, working with their doctors. She was approaching the last corner before the street where she was meeting Craig.

"Just one moment, Ms. Grace, and I'll check on that for you."

On what? Check on what? The sex of her child? Or whether there was anyone there who could give her that information?

She turned the corner. The parking lot they were

meeting in was half a mile ahead on the right. He might not be there yet. She was five minutes early. He was always there when she arrived. Always.

Maybe he was one of those people who had to be early everywhere they went. She couldn't stand to waste time waiting around. Nope, she was a right-on-time kind of person…her mind babbled, glommed on that which didn't matter…to distract her from that which did. Waiting was excruciating.

"Ms. Grace?"

She slowed as she approached the lot. Turned in. "Yes?"

"I have that information you wanted," the voice on the other end of the phone said as she parked and spotted Craig, standing between their two bikes.

"Okay." She was yards away from the sperm donor—the man who'd somehow become dear to her.

"You ready?"

Oh, God, get it done! "Yes."

"It's a girl, Ms. Grace! You're having a girl!"

A girl. *Isabella.* The name suddenly appeared, fully formed, in her mind.

A girl!

She was having a baby girl!

Looking down, Amelia cupped her stomach,

surprised when a tear dropped off her face, wetting her hand.

"I love you, little Isabella. I love you so much."

She wasn't just pregnant anymore. She had an unborn daughter.

Chapter Fifteen

Watching Amelia pull into the lot, Craig's welcoming smile dissipated when he saw her pull to a stop long before reaching him.

Leaving the bikes, he headed toward her car, concerned. Was she bleeding? Having contractions?

On the phone? he asked the questions silently, and with an oversized dose of self-disdain, slowing as he saw that she was in an active conversation.

He was about to turn around, to make it back to the bikes before she saw that he'd ever left them, before she knew he'd been rushing toward her, when he noticed her head move, her chin drop down to her chest.

At the car, he saw her hand rubbing her belly. She was crying.

His heart stopped. And then raced. He yanked on the door handle. It was locked. But she heard him, of course. Glanced up at him.

And that look on her face, beaming with something far greater than happiness, stopped the world from spinning. From turning at all.

She opened her door. "It's a girl," she said as she got out. "Her name is Isabella."

He wasn't sure how it happened, but she was suddenly in his arms and he was holding on. Tight. It was the first time they'd touched, other than hands passing over a bike, and the one brief kiss, and her body molded his. Thighs, stomach, chest to breast, her arms around his neck. He was in heaven. And the deepest of hells, too.

Because she was having a daughter, one that he'd helped create, but he would be sharing his life with neither of them: this beautiful woman nor the child she carried.

He held on. And then he let go. "You still want to ride?" he asked, getting himself firmly into his role in the moment. Finding his bedside manner— the one where he empathized, cared, but from a distance. He might play an intimate, prominent part during the moments his patients were with him, but he wasn't meant to be a part of their daily lives. He was a professional service. Not a personal relationship.

Whether or not he wanted more was irrelevant. Unless, or until, Amelia invited him in...

"Of course." Amelia sounded like she was on cloud nine as she walked beside him. And as though she knew that the situation was a little touchy for him, or maybe his lack of verbal response to her news had clued her in, she said, "Angie and I decided today to introduce some lace embellished baby clothes into our brand. We'll start out like we always do, with a few test pieces and go from there. Since we order in the basic pieces, and embellish by hand until an item is established, the initial cost will be minimal."

"So she's staying?"

"That's never been a question, according to her. I was the one making the offer more than it was."

She went to her bike—Tricia's bike, which Amelia was borrowing, he reminded himself—lifted the kickstand and stepped over the middle rail so she was straddling the bike between her legs.

Another moment and she'd have her foot on

the pedal, her cute butt on the seat, and she'd be heading off.

Craig stopped short of mounting his own bike.

"Congratulations," he said, looking her in the eye. "I'm proud of you for calling."

He was. And he was happy for her, too. Honestly. Maybe now he could begin the separation process. The letting go.

She nodded, still smiling. "I can't believe I waited for so long."

"People have a tendency to procrastinate when the results mean a lot to them," he offered. "Good or bad," he added.

"Yeah," she said, and broke eye contact, settled on the bike seat. "I shouldn't have waited so long."

She was talking about the results, about how she felt, having a daughter. And he watched. He couldn't let himself imagine how that felt. Wouldn't let himself. There was no good to come of doing so. Not until he had a family of his own.

And unless Amelia asked him to be a part of hers, he didn't yet have one, no matter how strongly he felt about her. And the baby girl she was carrying.

His daughter.

He led off with a hard push, yearning again

for the cliff trail he'd ridden hard the day before. Yearning harder. Yeah, it might be time to start letting go.

Less than five minutes into the ride, Craig slowed so they were side by side, and asked, "Is Isabella a family name?"

He'd been thinking about her, and her daughter, nonstop. Of course.

"No, why? Don't you like it?"

As in, it must be a family name or why else choose it? He hoped to God that wasn't what she'd thought he meant. He was just trying to stay on the outside looking in, while telling himself he shouldn't be looking in at all.

He knew that Isabella was going to be well cared for. Well loved.

His job was done here. Except that she'd asked a question. Where or not he liked the name she'd chosen. And…he was contributing to his daughter's health by giving her mother this opportunity to exercise. For another three or four weeks. Once she entered her third trimester, or grew enough of a stomach to change her balance abilities, they would stop.

So that's when he'd be done. Done with the job

he'd set himself—to ensure the well-being of his genetic offspring.

Right. Made sense. He couldn't let go just yet. But in a few weeks, he'd bow out for sure. And learn then how to live with the love growing inside him for both the mother and her child.

"I like the name," he assured her, feeling a weight lift off him as he reached his decision. He had a few more weeks to go. "I like it a lot, actually." He really did, when he allowed himself to think about it. "It sounds kind of royal, yet sweet, at the same time."

When she didn't say anything right away, he continued, "I just thought, by what you'd said on Sunday, that you weren't picking names yet." He hoped to God his asinine response to her news hadn't offended her. Made her doubt him.

He'd wanted to know. She'd given him a gift by telling him. She'd shared the news with him first.

And he'd reacted like a selfish ass.

"I didn't think I was. I mean, I think about them, but when I found out she was a girl, the name was just there, in my mind."

"I guess it's good that it wasn't a boy, then, huh? Isabella might not have worked as well."

"He was going to be Winchester," she said. "Win for short." She pedaled in silence for a few feet and then added, "I hadn't made a choice, really. They were just the names I liked best. When I thought about it."

And he understood. Giving up trying to control everything that could possibly hurt, letting herself believe that her dream was coming true, didn't miraculously happen upon realization. Just as he knew that, in spite of his feelings for her, he couldn't give up on his need to have a family of his own. With a woman who was married to him.

She'd made the call. She'd taken a step. She was trying to let go of her fear. Just as he knew he had to let go of her and their daughter—eventually.

The going wouldn't be easy.

It was right, though. Just as she knew what she needed to be happy, he did, too.

Neither one of them was wrong. They were just very different.

On opposite ends of a spectrum—joined by the spectrum—each with valid purpose. Destined to always be apart.

Almost as though Isabella understood that her mother had opened her heart, the baby kicked the very next day. Amelia was leaning over her drawing board, actually making progress, when the tiny disturbance hit her from underneath her skin. Right there at the surface of it, though. Or so it felt. In that first moment she just froze. Sat there suspended over the light board, her hand raised above the page, pencil dangling.

By late afternoon it had happened three more times. She'd run into Angie after the first time, but Isabella apparently hadn't want to share her accomplishment with her aunt. All three times Isabella had moved Amelia had been alone with her daughter. She found that telling.

And that was why texting Craig to tell him about the movement was wrong. She thought about it. From the first second of the first movement, she'd thought of him. Was painfully tempted. But she didn't give in.

She *couldn't* need him. Or turn to him for the big moments in her life, no matter how much her heart had begun to yearn for him.

And yet, those glimpses she was giving him of a child whose life he wasn't ever going to share seemed to mean a great deal to him. And was such a small thing for her to do, given the big picture.

She quarreled with herself about Craig all day Saturday, keeping busy with crib and nursery shopping, deciding on a theme of old-fashioned pink and white with teddy bears, choosing decals and paint colors.

On Sunday she and Craig were back at the parking lot at which they'd met for her very first bike ride. They'd never been back to his neighborhood, but when he'd suggested that they do that ride again, asked if she was opposed to it, she'd had no reason to disagree.

She found out why he'd wanted to take that particular route when she arrived to find a beautiful collie on a leash beside him.

"She used to always do my Sunday rides with me," Craig said as she approached, looking at the gorgeous animal she knew must be Talley. "She's doing so much better, so I wanted to give her a try today."

Which was why he'd needed to be in his neighborhood, she surmised. So Talley could be close to home if needed.

"You could have just told me that when you asked if I wanted to ride here again."

"I didn't want you to feel like you had to do so… if my area makes you uncomfortable."

"I don't feel like I have to do anything where you're concerned," she told him. Which was the whole point. He wasn't going to be that much of an entity in her life…right?

"Hey, Talley," she said, bending down to the dog, who was wagging her tail at Amelia. "You going to run with us today?" she asked, petting soft fur. Scratching Talley's neck. And laughing when the dog's tongue gave one short lick on her cheek.

She really should think more seriously about getting another dog. Tiki had added so much to their lives growing up. And she was settled now, had a place.

The first part of the ride was mostly silent. A few comments on Talley's ability to keep up, was all. She wanted to ride slower, for the dog's sake, but Craig kept up their usual pace until Talley showed signs of tiring.

"You did great, girl," he said, stopping his bike to give the dog a drink from a folding bowl he pulled out of a small pack on the back of his bike. Rubbing her head, her ears, he praised her as she drank.

It was the first time Amelia knew a human being could be jealous of a dog. And of a pat on the head. He was so tender, his hands so gentle, and...

"Do you mind if we stop by my place, drop her off?" he asked as he shook the bowl and put it back into the pack.

"Of course not." Truth was, she had to pee. She was drinking more as the weather warmed, and having to urinate with more urgency. But going into his home…

Shouldn't be an issue. They were friendly acquaintances. She trusted him implicitly. So why would it be a problem? He'd been in *her* home.

She fought with herself for the next block. They were traveling more slowly, for Talley's sake, and she figured if she could just keep riding she'd be fine. And then asked herself why she didn't just let herself go so she'd be more comfortable, why she was making herself suffer. She changed the subject back to being fine as long as she kept moving before she could answer herself.

In the end, her needs won out. As he stopped his bike at a three-car garage, next to a gate that led to the back of the property, and bent to unleash Talley, she asked him if she could use the restroom.

Of course he was immediately hospitable, letting the dog into the backyard, and taking Amelia into a laundry room not far from the back gate. Washer and dryer matched. And were clean. There were no clothes hanging on the bar in between the machines. Cupboards hung above them, holding the bar on either side.

"There's a bathroom right here," he said, showing her a door right outside the laundry room.

It was stupid to feel embarrassed for having to

relieve a bodily function. Everyone did it. Even Craig. And he was a doctor. Bodily functions were all in a day's work to him. He could probably tell her what parts went together, worked together to...

She was out of there as quickly as she could make it happen.

Craig wasn't standing nearby, thank God, and she went back outside, thinking she could play with Talley until he returned. She'd been right to refuse herself a bathroom visit. Being inside Craig's home was messing with her. Getting her all emotional and worried and het up and uncomfortable and...wanting more from him than she knew she needed.

No. She shook her head. Not wanting. Not really. She'd never been like this before, so easily aroused, sexually and otherwise, around anyone. Not even Mike. Not even in the beginning.

Talley was nowhere to be seen, but with more than an acre of trees in front of her, she wasn't all that surprised. Still, Talley had been tired, not likely to go play in the trees. It only took her a couple of seconds of looking to see the doggy door that led into the house farther down. Into a room she hadn't seen. One Talley was welcome to enter.

"There you are..."

She spun as Craig came out the same door

they'd entered through. "I was going to ask you if you'd like something to drink. Since we're here. I've got a fresh stash of juice."

She was going to say no, of course. She couldn't accept his hospitality. Seemed too personal.

While she fought with herself, her hormones answered for her. "I'd like that, thank you." It was rude to just leave the man standing there.

"You want to come inside?" He held the door.

She shook her head instantly. Brusquely. "I'll wait out here. It's lovely...all those trees."

He stood there for a second, studying her, and then went back inside.

He must think her an idiot. Or know that she was struggling. He had that peculiar ability to get into her head; he seemed to know her intimately.

No. She was making a mountain out of a mole-hill. And thinking in clichés now.

She had to stop this, all the internal fighting. She was a woman who took charge and maintained control. She knew better than to let her emotions play with her.

They'd lose. And she'd have to live with the mess they created. Clean it up. Take on more re-gret.

"You want to have a seat?" Craig was back, handing her a glass, and indicating the lovely patio, the wrought iron furniture boasting comfy-looking cushions.

She shook her head. Took a couple of steps farther into the yard. Talley came out and then went back inside.

"What's wrong?" Craig stood in front of her, his bottle of juice mostly empty. She'd barely sipped from hers, afraid it would choke her.

"Hormones," she told him. "It's all just hormones. I'm sorry. I'm not myself. We should probably go."

Instead of sending him heading for the gate, he stood unmoving, his brow furrowing with concern. Those eyes…how did fixtures in his face manage to convey such depth? And his hair—that wayward curl that hung just below his ear on the left side of his head. It was always there, just hanging out. Tempting her to touch it…

"What's wrong?" he asked again.

The truth? Isabella had moved and she'd wanted to call and tell him. Or text at least. And wanting that was bad. Wanting everything else—a man, a family together—was even worse.

He was a doctor. He'd know about these things.

Normal. She was normal. He'd understand.

"I'm just…" She took a sip from her bottle, relief flooding through her. "I've got the temporary hots for you," she said with a chuckle. Inviting him to chuckle along with her. "I know it's just hormones, but…how long does it last? Do you know?"

He wasn't chuckling. Or even grinning. He was staring at her, gaze intent. What…was he operating on her from the inside out now?

She wanted to look away. To move away. To drop her bottle of juice and run. She stood there, toe-to-toe with him, letting him do whatever he was doing: holding her captive with a look in his eye. And when his face moved, she lifted hers, still holding on to his gaze, watching him come closer.

His lips on hers was a foregone conclusion. She'd watched them approach. Read the intent in his eyes. She allowed the touch. Not pulling away as she had the first time their lips had touched.

Opening her mouth to him, she suckled hungrily. His arms came around her, pulling her fully up against his body. Her hands reached up to his neck, one still holding her juice as she clutched him like that, bottle dangling there, tasting fruit on his tongue. It was so good. *He* was so good.

The kiss was better than she'd imagined. His lips were gentle and masterful at the same time. Just like the man she'd come to know. Every part of her body trembled with wanting him. Wanting *more*. Her pelvis ached, pressing into him—and found his rock solid…paws landed on her shoulder before sliding between Amelia's upper arm and Craig's.

Because there would always be barriers between them.

The truth dawned suddenly on her. Amelia backed away.

"Oh, my God, I'm so sorry," she said, horrified with herself. How could she have…yeah, he'd been the first one to make a move, but she'd practically undressed right there in front of him, telling him what she needed. "I have to go…" She turned, hurrying toward the gate.

"Amelia." Craig caught up with her, stayed beside her as she continued forward, but didn't attempt to stop her. Didn't touch her. "It's okay," he said, but she knew it wasn't.

"And it most definitely wasn't your fault."

But it was. She was being selfish and maybe even cruel, inviting him to start something that she knew had nowhere to go.

She shook her head. Couldn't listen to him. Couldn't stay there. She had to get to her bike. His ex-lover's bike. The woman who'd originally owned and lived in this home with him. The home he intended to share with a wife and family. A home that made her feel trapped and afraid.

She had to get back to her car.

Because if she didn't, she knew she'd give in to fickle emotions and beg to stay.

Chapter Sixteen

Climbing on a bike with a hard-on was not pleasant. Nor was the fact that the woman who'd caused it could see full well that he hadn't controlled his desires around her.

His only comfort was that she wasn't looking anywhere in his direction and so, perhaps, had missed his evidence. Had she also missed the way his heart had started to pound when she'd returned his kiss?

He'd noticed how hers had.

He had to ride back to her car with her, to get Tricia's bike, but he'd have gone, anyway. They had issues between them to resolve.

And there was no way he'd have left her to ride alone—not as upset as she was.

Sliding down from the seat even before her bike had come to a complete halt, Amelia pulled her leg over the lower bar and had the kickstand in place before he'd dismounted. She yanked her keys from the pouch around her waist. "See you later," she said, turning toward her car.

Craig's bike tipped, almost fell over, as he hurried to follow her. He got to her just as she'd grabbed the driver's side handle.

"Wait," he said, just off to the side of her. "Please, Amelia. We need to talk."

"I don't want to talk."

"I'm not sure I do, either, but I think we should."

He knew as she stood there, hand on the door without opening it, that she was going to grant him his request. And knew instant regret.

He wasn't ready to say goodbye to her—or Isabella.

Would he ever be?

Two cars passed each other, pulling in and out of the lot. A nearby door slammed. He felt exposed. Far too public for the conversation ahead. And the bikes…

"I need to get the bikes locked up," he said. "We could talk in my vehicle. That way I'm not invading your space and you can get out and go at any time."

She didn't say anything, but followed him back to the bikes. Amelia rolled hers up alongside his SUV, waiting with it while he got his in the rack and then reached for hers. He'd already unlocked the doors and she climbed into the passenger side while he finished securing the bikes for the short drive home. He'd have taken longer if he thought she'd wait around.

He wasn't eager to hear her tell him that she couldn't see him again. That he couldn't see her again. If anything, he wanted the exact opposite.

"I should never have said anything about my overactive libido," she said before he'd even closed the driver's door behind him. Just hearing her say the word *libido* sent a shot of electricity right back to his genitals and he saw the error in his suggestion that they sit together in the vehicle. His body's instant reaction was right there up close and personal, for her to see. A hard-on and a steering wheel coexisting together.

There was just no good way to get out of the situation.

"I was just…you being a doctor and all…"

Yeah, adopting a bedside manner would have been good. Unfortunately, he wasn't at work, she wasn't a patient and the only visions he could see of her and a bed were of them in it together.

"I read that elevated sex drive was common."

"It is," he said. He had to say something. To make this right. "And you weren't wrong to talk to me about it," he added, not at all sure where to go from there. Except he said, "I'm the one who needs to apologize. I'm so sorry I took advantage of you. I wish I had a good explanation. I just don't."

"You didn't take advantage of me." She glanced over and their gazes met for the first time since Talley had interrupted them in the backyard.

He'd be giving the dog steak for dinner, or something comparable. She deserved all the thanks he could give her.

"I've been going crazy with wanting it to happen." She sounded disgusted with herself. And his body still rose to the occasion. Every time he'd start to relax, then there he was again, standing at attention. Just no easy way to do this.

"It's been on my mind, as well. And I'm not suffering from gestational hormonal fluctuations."

"We're diametrically opposed."

"I know."

"Your house...even being in the laundry room looking into the kitchen... I didn't want to be there."

"I kind of picked up on that."

"It's not just the house… It's… I don't want to get married, to be forever vulnerable to the actions of someone else."

"I know."

He hadn't asked her to marry him. Or even to go out with him. But he prudently held his tongue.

"You do."

"Yep."

"I know why this is happening. It's because I'm carrying your baby. Let's just put it right out there. That's the cause of the connection we're feeling. Right?"

He wanted to believe that was all it was.

"I mean, in a perfect world, there's supposed to be some kind of feeling associated with the whole your-seed-growing-inside-of-me process. That's what holds couples and families together. Or so I'm told. Sometimes."

"I can remember a time when I was kid," he said, looking inward. "I was about ten or eleven. I'd just done something good, though I've got no recollection whatsoever as to what it was. What I remember was the way my dad looked at my mom, and she at him, and then they both looked back at me with this identical smile on their faces.

I couldn't explain it then, but I felt so great. I've never forgotten that feeling."

He hadn't thought of it often, either.

"There was a bond there, because they were your parents," she said. "In your case, the bond probably solidified because they raised you together. In our case, we won't be...so an intense attraction between us—at least I know I'm feeling it and based on your struggle over there I'm guessing you're feeling it, too—will pass. Everything's new and unknown and pretty emotional right now, with this pregnancy and all. But when life settles back to a new normal, to a new routine..."

He wanted to believe her.

He wasn't sure he did.

But couldn't prove her wrong, either.

"It's possible," he told her.

Except...he had to be honest.

"Ever since you told me your baby is a girl... I keep thinking about Tricia. She had issues because her mother's married lover would never acknowledge her. And you and your sister...with your dad abandoning you and then Duane not filling that void. Both of you have been shaped so deeply by that. And now I've fathered a little girl who's going to grow up without a father in her life."

Her expression flattened and he knew he'd

scared her back inside again, to the place she went when she had to guard her heart.

"What are you saying? You want to coparent her now? To be—"

"No," he cut her off as her voice rose. "I've been honest with you from the beginning and I'm being honest now. In the first place, I have no grounds or rights to ask such a thing of you. And in the second, I told you I wouldn't. You've been good to me, allowing me this chance to get things right within myself. You've even said I could stay on the peripheries of Isabella's life as she grows, to be available if either of you ever need assistance that I can provide. I'm just telling you my thoughts. And…aside from Isabella, I'm just not sure that my attraction to you is going to dissipate as easily, or completely, as you think yours for me will."

"I'm not sure it will," she said, glancing down at her hands. "I'm just hoping it will. This increased sexual drive is all new territory for me."

He nodded, lips pursed as he watched a couple leave a dog in the car as they held hands and walked around the corner. It wasn't hot enough to be all that dangerous yet. But if they left the car long enough, with the way car interiors heated up in the direct sun, it could become dangerous.

He wasn't going to leave until he was certain the

dog was okay. Until he could try to make things okay between him and Amelia.

Not that he was trying to convince himself anymore that he cared for her the same as he'd care for any other living creature.

She definitely mattered more.

"You want to stop riding?" she asked.

Maybe they should. "Not really," he told her. "Though we're going to have to in another couple of weeks."

He figured she'd known it was coming just as he had. It was the first either of them had spoken of their imminent separation.

"We're diametrically opposed." They were back where they'd started.

"I know." He wished he could tell her he might be happy someday to pursue a relationship with a woman who just wanted to live together. But he knew better. His time with Tricia had taught him that. Taught him, too, that trying to fit into a relationship that didn't fit ended up stealing happiness from everyone.

"But it seems that we're going to be some kind of friends," she added, frowning as she peered out the front windshield. Whether she didn't like something she saw out there, or her expression was a result of inward sight, he wasn't sure.

"I hope we'll always be in touch," he agreed. A lot of times people parting ways said that and then never spoke again. But Isabella bound them.

"Feel free to tell me I've flipped my lid," she said, glancing him up and down and then turning toward her window. "Be prepared for me to tell you that and back up on what I'm about to say..."

And there it was. She intrigued him all over again. He was ready to say hello again, rather than the goodbye of seconds before.

"I'm listening."

"I was just thinking, since we both so clearly see that we don't belong together—not that anyone suggested we did—what's it going to hurt if we, you know, put ourselves out of our misery?"

Had she just suggested what he thought she had?

"Neither one of us would have to worry that the other was going to get hurt," she continued in the same conversational tone. "Or that we'd get hurt."

He wasn't sure life worked like that. If one could control one's ability to get hurt...

He had to stop this. To stop her talking.

"As I said at the beginning, feel free to tell me I've—"

"Stop." He glanced over at her. Leaned toward

her. Close enough that he could kiss her. Her lips were open as she met his gaze.

"What exactly are you suggesting?"

"That we have sex."

"Seriously?"

"Yes. Though, as I said, I might change my mind when I get home and think about what I'm doing."

"You want to do it right now, then? Right here?"

Her adorable head tilt, and her mischievous grin, almost got her her wish. "Of course not," she said. "I think we should set a time. And it should either be in a hotel or at my place. No offense, but your house wouldn't be a good choice for me."

That house she'd grown up in had really done a number on her. Made him want to grab up Duane whatever his name was, put him in a dark hole in the ground and leave him there until he'd felt every bit of insecurity and terror Amelia had known growing up with him.

"That way we both have time to think about it, and if either of us changes our mind, we're free to do so."

She wanted him to think about having sex with her. To have a date set. To anticipate the act…

The woman was going to drive him insane.

If he wasn't there already. "You have a date and time in mind?"

She gulped. Stared at him. And then, chin up, said, "No. I kind of thought you'd refuse."

"Do you want me to?"

"I should want you to."

"Do you?"

"No."

So they had that established. "I guess, then, we should set a date and time."

"Seriously?" She repeated his earlier word back to him, but in a far lighter, more delighted tone.

He shrugged, while his penis in the far-too-thin-and-revealing bike pants belied his relaxed response by standing up straight. Might as well be saluting. He glanced down at it.

"Seems pretty obvious that a date and time should be the next step," he told her, glancing over to find her looking at his crotch, and then up at him.

She grinned. "How about my place, an hour from now?"

"How about tomorrow night? At six. Your place if you'd like. And I'll bring dinner."

"You want time to think about it."

"I want us both to have time to think about it."

"You really think dinner's a good idea? It's not a date-date."

"We have to eat."

She nodded.

"Okay, then, tomorrow at six. At my place. You bring dinner." She opened her car door. "See you then."

She'd shut the door before he could respond.

So he sat there, openly watching her very stimulating backside as she made her way back to her car.

He was allowed to look. To appreciate. He was so hard he couldn't move. Had to calm his mind lest he explode.

And all it could think about was her. About exploding inside her.

There was no calming down. He and Amelia were going to have sex.

Chapter Seventeen

"I'm going to have sex with him." Amelia called her sister late that night. The conversation did not feel at all like something that should take place in the office the next morning.

Angie's silence hung over her, a heavy weight that hurt. She'd debated not telling her sister, but didn't want to feel like she was doing something she had to hide.

"It's just sex, Angie," she said now. "We're so different, wanting such different things in life… we both know we don't belong together."

Angie still didn't say a word.

"It's not me giving up myself," she said then,

starting to feel defensive when she knew she had no reason to do so. "On the contrary, for once I'm just taking what I want. I'm the one who suggested it. Only because I know he's on the same page," she added. "I'm not out to hurt anyone." Ever. Again.

"Then you should do it." Her sister didn't sound angry. Or even hurt. She didn't sound happy, either.

"You really think so?"

"I do."

"But you aren't happy about it."

Angie didn't respond. Amelia couldn't live to please her sister, either. Had never felt like she had to do so.

"Tell me why?" Her voice was pleading now, as she sat on her couch in the dark, wishing her sister was in the room with her. That they were kids again, in one or the other of their beds, whispering secrets when they were supposed to have been asleep.

Secrets girls their age shouldn't have known to whisper. Things drunken Duane had called them that they'd had to look up to find out what they meant. Worrying that they might be what he said.

"I'm afraid you're going to get hurt again," Angie said. "And I know that you can't stop being you, or needing what you need, and that if you don't reach for what you want, you will get hurt."

"Don't you ever yearn for things anymore, Angie?"

More silence.

"I'm never going to turn my back on you again. You know that, don't you?"

"Yeah."

"And you believe it?"

"Most of the time."

"I love you."

"I love you, too. Good night."

Angie hung up before Amelia could ask her younger sister to tell her what she yearned for and try to help her get it.

She was left with one other choice. To care. Be aware. Be present. And let the rest go.

But the subsequent long night showed her that the choice was easier thought than done.

Craig didn't change his mind. Granted, his job consumed all of his thought processes through most of the next day. But he wasn't having any trouble showing up at Amelia's building at a quarter to six on Monday night with a healthy dinner he'd purchased at the grocery store.

They'd never seen each other on a Monday before.

He'd almost put condoms in the bag, too, until he'd realized he wouldn't need them. He knew he was clean, and with her recent medical tests Amelia had just had done and shown him, he knew she was, too. And it wasn't like pregnancy was an issue. He did print out his recent medical results to give to her, just in case.

Condom-free sex. He'd never had it.

He'd never had sex with a pregnant woman before, either. But with his baby inside her…that part seemed kind of natural. And the rest of it—having sex when he knew there was no chance of building a relationship—he'd done it before. But not for many years. Not since before Tricia.

Amelia had given his name to the security guard—a different one from the previous time he'd visited her—and an elevator door opened the second he pushed the button. It took him up to her floor, the foyer of which was well lit. Someone had put a potted silk tree in the corner by the elevator. Not quite a backyard full of the real thing, but a nice touch.

Feeling a little empty-handed with just his bag of dinner, he knocked. Flowers, some kind of little gift, would have been more his style, to mark the occasion, the first time having sex, but this wasn't a date. Not in a traditional sense. It was more an... appointment.

He'd left on the dark pants he'd worn to work, changed his shirt and tie for an off-white pull-over. He was sure she'd have on her leggings and oversized T-shirt. Other than the first time they'd met, that was all he'd ever seen her in. It was all very practical.

He knocked a second time. With a tad more force. And got hard the moment she opened the door.

If it had not been for those gold-green eyes, he hardly recognized her. Her hair was down, waving past her shoulders, over breasts that were perfectly emphasized in a black-and-white dress stopped at the top of her thighs. The fabric had to be at least partially spandex, the way it hugged every curve of her body. Every curve. Including that baby bump.

Even it was a turn-on—that proof that his seed was growing inside her.

And she was wearing makeup.

"Wow." He didn't mean to speak aloud, but didn't stop himself in time.

Her grin made him glad he hadn't. "Thank you," she said, looking him in the eye. There was nothing shy or hesitant about her and he handed her the bag of food, then before she could dispose of it, took her in his arms, pulled her up against him and started kissing her like he was going to take her to bed right then. Full-on, tongue-engaged, body-pressing kisses.

He started to lose his thoughts when she pressed her body just as hard against his, her tongue engaging as eagerly. His hands couldn't stay still, running up and down her back, over her waist, learning the feel of her, finding that butt and holding on as he moved his crotch against her.

Her hand found his on her butt, covering it, holding him there, and then her fingers curled around his. A splash of cold dimmed his inferno as her body left his and she led him across the floor, around a corner, down a hall wider than his kitchen and through double French doors into a suite that felt luxurious, but all he really noticed was the queen-size bed.

He had no idea where dinner went. When or where she dropped the bag of food he'd brought. Didn't ask. Didn't care.

Her hands were at his waist, pulling at the bottom of his sweater. He helped, getting the garment up and over his head, dropping it on the floor. She looked at his chest—his form was something he was kind of proud of—and then up at him, her eyes glowing with all good things.

Her hands ran over muscles made firm and strong from staying active, her fingers tangling in his blond hair. When her fingers found his nipples, he gave a start. Wanted her tongue there. And bent to kiss her.

To slow things down before he embarrassed himself and ended their moment before it had really begun.

The man was Roman-statue gorgeous. Their clothes were gone—a mixture of her hands and his—and with one quick grab of his hand, the covers were thrown back. He lay back against pillows that until that moment had only touched her body, reaching for her and taking her entire weight as he laid her down, half on top of him, half beside him.

Neither of them had said a word since his "wow" and her "thank you" when she'd opened her door. She needed it that way and wasn't all that surprised that he seemed to, as well. She'd tried to talk herself out of taking him to bed, but the argument hadn't even gotten off the ground.

She needed to. He wanted to. No one was getting hurt.

She'd expected to be self-conscious, with her

body filling out in new ways since she'd become pregnant, her breasts heavier and more saggy than perky, but with the way he stared at her, as though he was seeing gold for the first time in his life, she felt completely comfortable. Beautiful, even. A heady sensation.

Her entire body hungry for his touch, she brought his hand to her chest, inviting him to her in every way, and reveled when he played with her, kissing her throat while his fingers rubbed her nipples. Turning, he laid her back and started a more thorough exploration, revering all of her— her chin, her neck, tracing her cheeks, staring deep into her eyes.

And then moved lower. His tongue followed his fingers on her nipples, both of them teasing her at once, and then he moved again, sliding lower. Spanning her ribs as he kissed the width of her, and then holding her hips as his mouth moved along her extended stomach. Kissing, dragging his tongue across her, sending chills up and down her entire body. Every part of her knew the touch of his tongue, the sexy glide of his fingers.

She almost stopped him when he reached the new curve of her belly, tensing at first, but the way he seemed to worship the small bump with gentle caresses and small kisses sent her spiraling to new levels of emotion, fueling her need to be consumed by the passion between them. To know it all. Do it all. Expel it all.

His journey to the hot spot between her legs was slow, tantalizing, teasing and gloriously frustrating as he moved on past it just as she was about to explode. Moving down one leg, up the other, he took time to savor every single part of her body, and when he moved up to cover her, trying to slide between her legs to enter her, she gave a push to his shoulder, guiding him back, intending to know his body, the taste and smell of him, as well as he knew hers.

To pleasure him as he'd pleasured her.

She got as far as the first nipple before he groaned. Gave her a pained look and, taking her hips in his hands, lowered her down on top of him, sliding into her with obvious struggle for control. His thumb found her spot as he filled her; suddenly, she exploded, her inner muscles clutching him, before he'd made a single thrust.

He never did make one that first time. Her body had barely covered his before he came, seconds after she did, with an animalistic "ahhhh" sound that she knew she was never going to forget.

He stayed inside her when they were done. Rolled with her so they were side by side, kissing her deeply, touching softly—her cheeks, her breasts, moving on to her nipples. Before she realized his intent, he was completely hard again, and she was on her back, with him thrusting in and out of her, creating extraordinary sensations she'd never known. She came without any external stimulation, wave after wave of sensation that had her sucking in her lower lip to keep from crying out. He followed immediately afterward, holding himself deep inside her as she still pulsated around him. And then they lay there, almost reverently. Not speaking, and yet…connected by more than just their bodies. She knew a sense of rightness she'd never experienced, a sense of being right where she was supposed to be, and, as their breathing settled, she dozed off.

Well, that had been the best sex of his life. Why he was still conscious, though, Craig had no idea. He lay in Amelia's bed, clearly welcome to drift off since the bed's owner was asleep half on top of him, staring at the shadows in a room illuminated only by the lights left on in other parts of the condo.

He thought about dinner. The chicken that, after two hours at room temperature, would no longer be safe to eat. And soggy broccoli salad.

He thought about Talley. About her at home alone, waiting for him before she'd jump up on his bed and settle into sleep.

Went through his schedule for the next day— lighter than usual as he had a couple of meetings to attend. One a monthly meeting of all the partner doctors in the clinic. And another with a pharmaceutical company.

What he tried not to think about was Amelia Grace and where she and her baby fit into his life. Or rather, didn't fit.

How could that be when she fit into his arms so well?

Kind of surprised at how quickly his body was springing back to life, just from the warm weight of her against him, he knew he had to get up and go. But was loath to attempt to extricate himself from the limbs tangling with his.

He could slide her top half onto the pillows behind him, and then one at a time get his legs free and off the bed. Or maybe if he slowly got one leg free first, so he'd be more stable, more steady, he could then do her torso and then his other leg. Yeah, that would probably work best. If he kept his arm under her neck and around her shoulders until the last minute...

A small jab in his side interrupted the plan.

Her hand? They were located on either side of his chest. The touch came again. Clearly there. And yet light. Nothing he could associate with a body part. Or digestive flatulence.

When it dawned on him, all departure plans fled. His feet were on the floor, his body bolt upright.

"What's wrong?" Amelia sat up, seeming to take in the situation with a second's glance, grabbing the sheet to cover herself. "Oh, I'm so sorry. I feel asleep on you…"

"You're okay," he quickly assured her, reaching for his pants. He had to get out of there. To get home. Back to his own world. To figure out what the rest of his life was going to look like and start heading in that direction. He shoved his boxers into his pocket.

"I'm just going to go," he told her. Their appointment had concluded. Their meeting was done. "I wouldn't eat the chicken if I were you." Wherever it was. He found his socks. Shoved them into the pocket with boxers, leaving them all half hanging out down his thigh. "It's been too long at room temperature."

"Okay. Are you…should we not have done this?"

"Yes. Yes, we should, and I'm fine. Just need

to get home." His shirt on, he rearranged the socks and boxers, stuffing them into three different pockets, so that they'd be fully contained, not sticking out when he walked in front of the security cameras between her bedroom and his SUV in the visitor parking lot outside. "Where do you want to meet tomorrow and what time?" he asked.

It was their usual goodbye—setting up the next ride. And all he had at the moment.

He needed a hot shower.

A beer.

A conversation with his dog.

He absolutely did not need to replay, ever again, his daughter's touch against his side. "It's a shorter day for me…" she started when he asked her about their next bike ride. She was going to cancel. He'd thought about it, too. But didn't want to let it go yet… "So…is it okay with you if we do the college campus again?"

"Yes. Four-thirty?" He grabbed the lifeline before she could change her mind.

She hadn't left the bed, but he knew from her frown that she was confused. At the very least. He had everything he needed, even his shoes on bare feet.

"Yeah. Four-thirty's good."

"See you then." With a quick nod, he was out of there.

Chapter Eighteen

She felt like she'd just lost her best friend. Scrambling an egg to eat with a piece of dry toast, Amelia caught a whiff of chicken from the garbage can where she'd deposited the bag Craig had brought, which she'd dropped on the floor just outside her door as she'd taken the man to bed. The thought of it made her cry.

So she went around the house collecting trash from all of the other cans, tied the drawstrings and, in brightly colored floral pajama pants and a T-shirt, she walked the bag out to the chute in the elevator foyer.

By the time she got back, her eggs had started to

congeal in the pan. She added a little milk. Stirred them vigorously, let them cook another second and then ate them straight out of the pan.

You did what you had to do to feed the children. That was a rendition of a line from one of her favorite books recommended at some point during her years of counseling. She had a child to feed, so she ate congealed eggs when all she really wanted to do was curl up in her sheets, smell the man who'd been in them with her and watch television.

He'd cut out of there like a bat out of hell. Which had been the right thing to do. They weren't in love. Having a relationship. They'd made an appointment to have sex. And they'd been done. It was the wasted chicken and salad that made her weepy. Chicken and hormones.

Craig made sure they had a ride time and place established before he left.

He wasn't done with her yet.

She took that thought to the living room couch where she pulled a blanket over her tender and still-buzzing body, shoved a throw pillow under her head, turned on the television and started to cry.

Craig spent a good bit of the night concerned about Amelia. Hoping his abrupt departure hadn't upset her, too much. Knowing it had.

Talk about "wham-bam, thank you, ma'am." What an ass he was.

And he thought a lot about Isabella, too. Trying to figure out where she fit into his world. Could he really just walk away with only occasional tidbits? And the reality was, he had no other choice. No legal recourse if Amelia wouldn't allow more. Would he be content, at peace, just with the knowledge that Amelia could call if she needed him? Could he trust that she would?

He asked the hard questions. Got no definitive answers.

Except one. He had no choice.

He had no rights, no power, to change any of it even if he wanted to do so. Nor would he even try. Amelia had opened her life to him in good faith. She'd trusted him not to try to insinuate himself into her child's life. He had to honor that trust, at least.

Half thinking she wouldn't be at their designated spot on Tuesday, he loaded the bikes and showed up, anyway. He was a show-up kind of guy.

And one who allowed himself to be relegated to the sidelines of life.

The thought stopped him cold, Tricia's bike suspended over his head on its way down from his SUV in the parking lot.

He'd allowed himself to be pushed aside with Tricia and as a by-product, Gavin. And he was doing it again with Isabella. Not that he could have forced either woman to share their children with him. Nor would he want to do so.

But the realization told him something key about himself. He seemed content to be on the sidelines.

His work required him to focus on a person's health, and then step aside as the family processed the emotional aspects of what he shared—good and bad.

But as he lowered the bike, he had a sudden vision of the way he had figured into Tricia's life. She'd said she wasn't open to marriage and he'd allowed himself to settle for less than he wanted. He'd wanted to adopt Gavin, or have some kind of guardianship rights, but when Tricia had demurred, he'd continued to live with them. To be a father figure to the boy—without any say in any of the key decisions in Gavin's life. Tricia had made all of those, from what sports he'd play to new school clothes.

Craig's bike came down next.

And yeah, what was he supposed to have done? Walked out? Left the boy to fend for himself? And Tricia…

So, maybe he hadn't loved her as much as he'd once thought he had...

His bike bounced down to the ground with a bit too much force as that thought reared. Of course he'd loved Tricia.

As much as she'd let him.

Amelia wasn't letting him love her at all.

But he did. A rush of emotion swamped him as he thought of her sleeping in his arms the night before, and had him wiping his forehead on his sleeve. He'd never felt anywhere near that intensity of feeling for Tricia.

He'd learned some things. Matured.

He knew he couldn't settle for less than he needed.

Just as he knew that Amelia couldn't, and shouldn't even try to, give more than she had to give.

The only question left...where did that leave them?

She'd just pulled into the parking lot.

Thank God.

Tuesday's ride was like any other weekday excursion they'd taken. Shorter than Sunday. Less talking. Afraid that she'd damaged her friendship with Craig after what had happened last night,

Amelia gave everything she had to pretending that nothing had changed.

Because, in a very real way, nothing had.

Yeah, she was struggling a bit more with keeping her hands off him, struggling not to think about the chest underneath that spandex shirt and the rest of him…tucked inside those tight pants. Her mouth got a little drier as they rode, and she had to access her water bottle a bit more often.

She tried to picture herself living in Craig's house with him—even just as a live-in girlfriend, not a wife—and her insides cramped. Like bad was just around the corner. Walls of worry. *Her* worries.

She'd known a woman in group counseling who had the same reaction to Sundays. Something had happened to her on a Sunday afternoon as a child. Football had been on at the time. And thirty years later, that woman still had to fight feelings of oppression on Sunday afternoons, most particularly during the fall months.

Emotional memory, their counselor had explained, adding something to do with hormones and brain chemicals that are triggered…

The big home, the yard, so privately offset from anyone else in the world—all that sent her spiraling. It just wasn't right for her.

And wasn't something she was likely to grow out of.

And when she pictured a life without Craig in it?

It wasn't good, either.

Was there some other therapy she could try?

Wasn't the love more important than *where* they shared it?

She'd done a real number on herself with this one. Had no clear way out. And all she knew was to continue to move forward. Take the next step. And then the next.

When she had to say goodbye to him, at least as a weekly occurrence in her life, a way would be made known to her.

They finished that Tuesday's ride in near-silence. Neither of them brought up anything about the night before, good or bad. As she handed over the bike to Craig, Amelia tried to catch his eye, but only once. Briefly. She didn't succeed and didn't try again.

"What time Thursday?" she asked him.

He suggested they meet at five in the parking lot closest to her building—since they were starting later than usual. She'd have agreed to meeting on a mountaintop if he'd suggested it. Nodding, she waited until the bikes were secure and, when he turned, his biceps bulging, she told him good night.

Hard to believe that the night before she'd been lying naked in her bed with those arms wrapped around her. Hard not to be hurt by his abrupt departure and subsequent behavior.

Harder still to convince herself that she wouldn't do it all again.

Craig went to Thursday's bike ride ready to have "the talk." The "we need to talk" kind. Enough was enough.

He'd started this whole thing—spending time together while trying to avoid building some kind of relationship. Time that was designed to remain completely impersonal as far as the two of them were concerned. Hard to remember exactly why he'd thought it a good idea. Or even how he'd thought it could work.

Sometime over the past two days he'd reached the conclusion that they'd need to discuss their situation instead of ride. Still, he had the bikes on top of his SUV when he pulled into the lot, surprised to see Amelia already there.

That couldn't be good. She'd never been early by more than five minutes before, and it was a good ten before their designated time.

"We need to talk," she said, standing not far from his car. "I was thinking maybe we walk instead of ride? Or ride and then walk?" She glanced up at the bikes.

"Let's do that," he said, reaching for his bike. "Ride, then walk." He harrumphed as he unhooked the bike and lifted it down. Him thinking they needed to talk was one thing. He could control his own imagined outcome.

But who knew what ideas she had in her head? He couldn't control Amelia's thoughts.

He needed some bike time to prepare to hear them.

Half a block down the road, he slowed, waiting on the quiet neighborhood street for her to catch up with him. Most homes had lights on. A lot had cars in the driveways. None had kids outside. It was dinnertime.

"Look, if you're regretting Monday, don't. It happened. We can get by it," he said.

"I wasn't regretting Monday." She didn't look at him. He knew. He'd glanced at her. Slowed even further, lifting up straighter with only one hand on the handlebar. "Unless you are, I guess. If it was wrong for you, then I regret it."

"No!" he blurted like an imbecile into the

street. "I don't regret it. Other than it seems to have cramped our style some."

"Yeah, that's what I wanted to talk to you about." She looked at him then, but he couldn't read the expression in her eyes. Whether she'd purposely worn her helmet lower, or it had slid down, he didn't know, but he didn't like how it shadowed her face and hid the things he needed to know. "So…you have no regrets? It was good for you, too?"

That "too" about had him almost falling off his bike. "Yeah." There was an embarrassing wealth of weight in the one word.

She nodded. Pedaled.

That was it?

She had nothing more to say? Just needed to know that he'd enjoyed himself in her bed? So like her to tend to his pleasure. And so damned infuriating, too.

But he couldn't really be angry with her, especially not since he'd left her bed without even staying to say goodbye the morning after. Amelia was playing by rules he'd agreed to. Rules he'd helped establish. She was keeping them on a track upon which they could both ride.

He could get off at any time. He was the one who'd pushed his way in. The choice was all his.

"We've only got a couple of weeks left of safe riding," he said, thinking about her stomach. Her balance. For the previous two days he'd done all he could not to think of Isabella. Of his daughter's tiny touch.

"Yeah."

"I guess we settle into a place where you call me if you need me after that," he continued. He had to take control. Move on, even if he didn't know quite yet where he was going. Ahead, he knew that. The practice was going well. He still felt passionate about his job. He just needed to start getting out more. Getting involved in things that weren't work related.

For the first year after Tricia's death, he'd been consumed with fighting for Gavin. And during the second, while he'd been waiting for state supreme court dates, he'd come out of his grief enough to start dating.

Now, he could get on with finding the love of his life. Starting a family. He had to do so for his own sanity. He could *not* spend the rest of his life loving Amelia.

"I'm happy to stay in touch, Craig."

Her words could mean anything from thrice weekly meets as they were doing now, to once every couple of years, as he'd at first envisioned.

"I'm really going to miss these rides," she added.

He'd still be riding. But he was going to miss her—and still love her—despite his silence.

Something was bothering Craig. Amelia was driving herself mad trying to figure out what it was. Because that's what she did…made life about another person.

Because it was the right thing to do.

The non-selfish thing to do.

Because if she didn't please, others weren't going to love her.

Words from a counseling session years ago came back to her out of nowhere. Her therapist had told Amelia that her mother acted in a similar way when it came to the men in her life. Amelia had learned from her.

Amelia had done everything Mike had asked, even when it had seemed wrong to her, to prove her love. To earn his love. She knew all that.

But she didn't love Craig. And didn't expect his love.

Did she?

She just cared about him as a person. Because he was decent. Kind. Generous. Patient. Gentle. And there was some extra connection there because his donation had given her the ability to live her best life. To have her family. To be complete.

And he really just needed to be at peace with Isabella's future. Like his other female recipient, the ten-year-old in Oregon. He'd move on to his own life when this was done.

Thoughts swirled around as she circled with Craig back to the parking lot where they'd left their vehicles. She was heading to Angie's for dinner and to look for baby things on the internet, things they'd then order in bulk from manufacturers for apparel and amenities to add to the infant division of Feel Good. And if she found some cute outfits, she might have to get them for Isabella.

By the time they'd stopped at his SUV, she knew she couldn't just leave, in spite of the fact that Angie was waiting.

"Would you please tell me what's wrong?" Hands at her sides, she stood directly in front of him.

He shook his head, as though he was going to deny being bothered, and it occurred to her that it might not be about her at all. He could have a patient with a scary diagnosis. Something he wasn't at liberty to share. What a self-centered little girl she was, making everything about her.

"Monday night changed things for me."

Talk about her worst nightmare coming true. Well, not the worst. Not by far. She had her family. Isabella was thriving. They might be adding a baby division to the business...

"Okay." She had to handle this. She'd started them down that path. "How do we fix it?"

He put his bike up, secured it, leaving her hanging there.

"I don't know that we do," he said when he was facing her again.

"Wow." She met his gaze, and then couldn't. "Okay." She could handle this. She *would* handle it. "Are you breaking up with me?"

As soon as she heard the words, she knew they were the wrong ones. They weren't even together.

But she felt like she was in the middle of the worst breakup ever.

Maybe it was hormones, this feeling of desperation climbing inside her. *Please God, let it be hormones.* Could they suck the air out of you?

"I don't know what I'm doing." Craig's words, delivered in that familiar, confident tone, put breath back into her lungs. Enough to fight for something that had no name.

"We're kind of in a mess here, I know," she said. "Me, a single mom being friends with my sperm donor. And you...a responsible man needing to ensure that your biological offspring is well." She glanced up at him, full of energy when he looked straight at her. "But so what?" she said. "Who says we can't be friends? That we can't make this work? If I want it, and you want it, it's up to us, isn't it? It's no one else's business."

"You want to remain friends."

"Yeah, don't you?"

"I do," he said, his gaze serious. "But…"

She didn't like "buts." Never had. Neither did Angie. Too many times that word had come out of their mother's mouth in the most critical moments.

She shook her head.

"We can't keep pretending we don't care about each other," he finished.

Tears sprang to her eyes. At the absolutely worst moment. "Agreed," she said.

He continued to look her in the eye, sending her comfort and a whole slew of other feelings. Leaving her with questions that didn't have answers.

"I have a few close friends I really care about," she said. "Don't you?"

"I do." The doctor who'd brought him to Marie Cove in the first place, who was now a current partner in his firm, she remembered. "But I don't have sex with them."

"We only did it once." Two friends of hers in

college, suitemates, had done it once after a night of drinking. She'd walked in on them. It happened. It was over. No big deal. They were both married now, to other people, and still friends.

"I want to do it again."

Understanding dawned with a relief that made her dizzy. He had the hots for her body.

"There's no law that says we can't. For now. Until it doesn't work for one or the other of us."

What was she saying?

She couldn't have sex with him without commitment, could she? But hadn't she already? She was going to live her life without a committed partner, but she did intend to have sex again.

"I'd need it to be monogamous, just because anything else gets too complicated, and it opens the risk for the passing on of things," she continued, blabbering on as she tried to think. Trying to keep talking so he couldn't immediately take the option off the table.

"We already know we aren't suited for anything more and both of us feel that way, so we're going into it with our eyes open. And for now, while there's no one else either of us want to sleep with, why not? We're both adults." She couldn't seem to shut up.

Maybe she should have stopped before the stupid clichés started spurting out.

"This is something you want? Not something you're agreeing to, to keep me happy?" he asked.

Like she said, they were friends. He knew her and had her back.

And she knew him, his sense of responsibility.

"I've been trying since Monday to figure out how I could possibly ask you to do me a favor and do that to my body again," she said. "Because while it worked for the moment, it was so good it just made my hormones rage harder."

His grin made her belly flop. "That good, huh?" he asked, his expression all male.

She smiled at him, tempted to kiss him and show him how ready she was, but knew she had to get to her sister. And didn't want to show up all hot and bothered.

Growing serious, she said, "I don't know if this is a good idea or not," she said, "but I know it sounds like the right solution in my head. As long as we're honest with each other. When you meet someone you think you want to date, or are ready to go find your wife, you tell me immediately. And if, after I have the baby and my hormones level out and I don't want to have sex anymore, I tell you. Or, after I have the baby, we stop so it doesn't complicate things with her."

"Or anything else in between," he added. "If it complicates things anytime, we stop."

"Agreed."

A glint came into his eye. "You busy tomorrow night?"

"No."

"Your place or mine?" he asked. And then held up a hand. "Your place," he answered for her. "And I'll forgo the dinner."

Right. Because they weren't dating. But…

"We can order in," he finished.

"But…" This was getting complicated already.

"You ever eat with your friends, Grace?" he asked, his use of her last name making her chuckle. She was making trouble where there was none. Or maybe she just didn't want to see it lurking there.

"I'll see you tomorrow night," she told him, and turned her back before she screwed things up.

So their relationship wasn't conventional. Angie wasn't going to be happy about it, that was for sure. And maybe her sister had cause for concern. After all, Craig was eventually going to meet someone else and get married, while Amelia was going to be a single mother for the rest of her life. No way was she going to take a chance that Isabella would suffer from her issues as she and Angie had suffered from their mother's. She had some definite blind spots. She struggled to trust herself emotionally, which hindered her ability to communicate what she was feeling sometimes.

So yeah, maybe she was going to get hurt.

And maybe, since she was the only one who would, she was willing to take that risk.

Chapter Nineteen

That next Friday night turned into three more just like it. With Wednesdays and Sundays thrown in in between them. Instead of meeting in parking lots, they were meeting at Amelia's home, and instead of riding bikes, they were riding each other.

They'd have sex, with a little talk, and he'd always get up and leave her bed immediately following the act. He also kept himself from as much immediate contact with her burgeoning belly as he could. Tried not to think of the little girl growing there.

Craig couldn't fall in love with the baby, too, any more than he already had. She wasn't his.

Sometimes they ate together. A lot of times not. As though by mutual decision they weren't spending much more time together than they had before.

He knew enough about the body and relationships to know that eventually passion would dim somewhat with familiarity and repetition. He told himself that when it did, they'd spend less and less time together. They'd drift back to their own lives, with occasional contact pertaining to Isabella's welfare. Maybe he'd get school updates once in a while. Or have the chance to glance over medical records.

It wasn't going to be enough. None of it was enough.

But he couldn't walk away. No matter what the future brought, Amelia was someone he was never going to forget. And Isabella would always be a part of him.

He still hadn't met Amelia's sister. They hadn't done anything together outside their predetermined appointments for physical exercise. He kind of liked it that way. The more people who came into their sphere, the more judgment there'd be. The more pressure. And questions.

He shied away from the possibility of questions most of all. Mostly because he knew them all and had no answers. He was a doctor. A healer. And couldn't find his own cure.

And for the most part, he was fine with the arrangement for the time being. He'd spent a Saturday night with his folks and didn't like not telling them that there was going to be a little girl named Isabella born with their genes. It would kill them to know they were going to be grandparents with no rights to see the child, which was one reason why he'd never mentioned the other child in the world carrying his genes. That one they'd understand more easily, in that the girl had loving adoptive parents, a complete family. They'd never in a million years understand his relationship with Amelia. Standing on the outskirts of the family, but not being a part of it.

He wasn't sure he understood it himself. But it was working. He was happier being in her life than outside it. And she made it very clear that his visits were the highlight of her week.

Her belly was growing noticeably, but neither of them spoke of the baby she carried, other than a brief mention that she'd had a monthly checkup and everything was fine. And that had come only because she'd had to be a little later than usual one Wednesday night due to the after-work obstetrical appointment.

If she had a nursery prepared in her home, she didn't mention it to him, and he purposely didn't look. They had clearly established boundaries between them and they were both sticking to them as religiously as they were sticking to each other. He didn't know about her, but for his part, he didn't want to do anything that would rock their boat even a little bit.

It would happen at some point. She was going to deliver her baby and everything would change. She wouldn't be free for three nights a week of dinnertime sex, for one thing. Unless she hired a babysitter, she wouldn't be free for much of anything.

And maybe that would be the time that he met someone else and started his own life. Maybe this was only meant to last throughout gestation. He'd get to experience this beginning of his daughter's life, to be with Amelia through her pregnancy, and then move on to start his own family. He'd be able to let Isabella go then. Just as he had with the Sanders family in Oregon.

He clung to the logic in that as, night after night, he poured himself into Amelia, holding on as though he never had to let go.

But he knew he did. And that when the time came, he would.

* * *

Amelia loved being pregnant. She loved feeling her daughter move inside her, sharing her body. Loved being a part of the miracle of creation. Of knowing that she was helping to bring a human being into the world—someone who might grow up to make the world a better place.

And she loved the passion she felt in Craig's arms, night after night. Who knew hormone surges could provide such a wonderful side effect?

She'd figured the way he made her body buzz would fade, but as weeks passed she craved him more, not less.

Lying in his arms one Wednesday night, having just exploded with an orgasm that went on and on, she wished he'd just spend the night for once. She needed to sleep and didn't want to wake to find him gone.

Snuggling against his naked body as he lay on his back beside her, she rested her belly up against his side, finding his support of the weight rather nice, and closed her eyes.

Just as she was drifting off, Isabella jabbed her a good one about an inch below her right rib. There'd be another one or two, and then the baby would settle, she knew. The pattern was becoming pretty regular, almost as though the baby was telling her good night...

"I gotta go."

Before she'd even comprehended the meaning of his words, Amelia was lying naked and alone with the cold breeze left by Craig's abrupt departure from the bed. He was stepping into the beige shorts he'd worn. A black, short-sleeved shirt half hung off the end of the bed.

"Wait."

He buttoned and zipped his shorts, reached for his shirt. She grabbed it.

"What's wrong?" she asked him. So she'd been reaching a bit, thinking he might stay. She knew he had to get home to Talley. But he also didn't usually jump out of bed so fast that she felt as though she'd been dumped. Not since that first time.

"Nothing. Come on, give me my shirt."

She lifted it to her breasts, covering them. He turned, clearly avoiding her.

"Look at me," she said. "Please."

When he did, her whole being settled into a sense of foreboding. "Craig?"

There was pain in the shimmery glint in his eyes, in the tightness around his mouth.

"What's wrong?"

"Nothing."

"Don't lie to me. We said this would only work if we were honest with each other. What's going on? Did you meet someone?"

Dread filled her, a painful weight starting to bloom in her chest. She'd known it was going to happen. Was prepared for it to happen. But had put off dealing with it until the baby was born. Somehow, in her mind, she'd settled into the idea that she had Craig until after Isabella came.

He looked at her, but didn't answer.

"Did you?" she asked, and then, forcing into her voice a lightness she absolutely didn't feel, said, "Because if you did, it's okay! You just need to tell me. We'll still be friends, and you can get whatever updates you want or need on Isabella."

"Give me my shirt."

She handed it to him, getting up to grab a pair of lightweight sweats and a T-shirt, pulling them on as she followed him out to her living room.

"Please don't leave like this." She had tears in her voice, and her eyes. "I understand if you're done. But... I don't...we said we were friends..." And then it dawned on her. "She doesn't want me in your life, is that it?"

It made sense.

"No!" He turned, anger in his voice. "That's not it, Amelia. There is no 'she.' There's no one. I told you, everything's fine. I just need to get home. I have a long day tomorrow. An early appointment."

Perhaps a difficult diagnosis. Or hard news to impart. She wanted to believe that was all it was.

But he hadn't given any indication when he'd arrived that evening that anything was amiss. It wasn't until...

She thought back... She'd been falling asleep—which wouldn't have upset him, would it? They'd both dozed before for a few minutes when their coupling had been particularly energetic—and satisfying.

There'd been nothing... Isabella had said good night and...

He'd flown out of bed.

She stared at him.

"You felt her kick."

His nostrils flared, his lips tightening. "I told you, it's nothing."

But it clearly was.

As Amelia stood before him, asking him not to leave, Craig thought to himself that he'd come off a hard day—nothing critical, just a flu going around with a crowded office of people who didn't feel well and didn't need to be waiting to get in to see him. A day when his PA had called off at the last minute for similar symptoms.

And he did have a full schedule the next day, starting with an early appointment to accommo-date one of the first patients he'd ever had—a young man who was now in college and commut-ing to LA every day for classes. He needed a sports physical and didn't want to see anyone but Craig.

"This is hurting you."

He could continue to deny the truth. To lie to her. And it would serve no purpose. She'd fig-ured it out.

"Life hurts, Amelia. You know that. There's no avoiding it. So yes, sometimes…maybe more lately…it's hard sometimes. But being with you, great sex aside, is one of the best parts of my week. I look forward to seeing you. I'm just tired to-night. I need to get home and spend a little time with Talley before bed. Everything will be fine in the morning."

"No," she said, her nose only inches from his chin as she lifted her face to look him right in the eye. "We said this was only going to continue as long as it worked. But it's not really, is it? This isn't like that little girl in Oregon, with two parents in a happy family. You're starting to bond with Isa-bella, aren't you?"

"No." He met her gaze full-on. "And that's what's hard sometimes. Remembering that she's not mine to bond with."

"You want her to be yours."

He didn't want to get into it. Not then. "No," he said again, and glanced over her shoulder, needing a breather. Then looked back at her. "I want her to be yours, Amelia." Lifting a hand, he smoothed a strand of her long, silky auburn hair back behind her ear. Hair that had been splayed across his naked body less than an hour before. "I care about you," he told her. "I'm glad that I'm the one giving you your family. That I'm the one who helped make your dreams into reality." Complete truth. He just wasn't sure it would be enough.

She shook her head. "No, this has to stop," she said, backing away from him. "If I'm hurting you, it has to stop."

"Amelia, don't do this."

"I have to." She had tears in her eyes again. "I can't knowingly hurt you. Because I care, too, Craig, and it's not right for me to continue to take my pleasure at your expense."

She could have just been talking about the sex. He knew she wasn't.

"I'm a grown man. I can take care of myself."

"Then do it," she said.

Then do it. That was coming from a woman who'd given up self to please the one she was with. Three simple words that made everything clear.

Being around her was the highlight of his week. And the lowlight, too. Because he was kidding himself. He wasn't ready to walk away. He'd never be ready.

She was the woman he loved. And she was carrying his daughter.

She came toward him again, slowly, holding his gaze the whole time. His heart softened, as though for a second it held hope. Lifting up, she kissed him. A kiss unlike any they'd shared.

There was no passion. Just a promise of good thoughts, of connection and kind regard always. She was kissing him goodbye.

"Please, please call if I can help in any way," she said, stepping back.

That was his cue. He nodded. "Will you do the same?"

She nodded.

"Honestly?"

"I swear, Craig. It's the least I can do for you. You can rest assured that if you don't hear from me, she's fine."

"And you," he said. "I…care, Amelia. If you

ever need anything, if there's anything I can do to help, I want you to call. It would make me happy."

She nodded, her lower lip trembling, and turned, heading slowly down the hall, clearly leaving him to let himself out.

He stood there, watching his family walk out of his life, wanting to go after them. Wondering if he was making a mistake. And knowing he wasn't. A break now was hard. But after Isabella came and life settled into something that wasn't right for either of them, a break would still come. And it wouldn't be just the two of them hurting then. It would be Isabella, too.

Grabbing his keys, he left.

Chapter Twenty

Amelia cried for a while after Craig left. She cried for a life she couldn't have. Cried because she'd hurt him. And hurt herself again, too, even after swearing to herself that she wouldn't let it happen. Because she couldn't make things better for them. Because she missed him already. And then she lay in her bed, her head where his had been, her hand on her belly, and took comfort from the fact that it was his daughter growing inside her.

She'd looked at a lot of profiles of potential sperm donors—all were good ones. The Parent Portal screened very carefully. She could have picked any number of them.

She was so thankful she'd chosen him. And fell asleep telling herself that everything was going to be all right.

The "breakup" hurt in the moment, but she and Craig would both be fine. They'd known their time together wasn't going to last forever. With a little time to get some distance and perspective, they'd be fine. Able to talk on the phone now and then, keep up with each other's lives.

She went to sleep feeling somewhat better. But she woke up with a cloud that followed her everywhere and continued for days. No matter what she did, where she was, what she told herself or did to distract herself, she couldn't shake the darkness.

And if she gave in to it, she cried. Which was how Angie found her the following Tuesday afternoon, six days after Craig had walked out of her life forever. Sitting at her drawing table, a necklace design that had been going well and then nowhere, ruined by her tears.

She'd told her sister about Craig leaving the morning after it had happened. Angie had been great, holding her while she cried, crying a little with her. Listening to her. She'd never once said "I told you so."

Instead, Angie had told Amelia that she had

done the right thing because she'd listened to herself and followed her own heart.

Amelia told Angie that she didn't regret her time with Craig. She was so glad she knew him. So thankful that Isabella's father was such a great, decent and kind man.

"Come here." Angie took her hand, led her from the drawing board to the couch, sitting down with her and then jumping back up to get her a small container of juice from the minifridge. She grabbed one for herself, too, uncapping one and handing it to Amelia and then taking a sip of the other for herself.

"I think you need to reassess," Angie said, her tone kind but sure. In black jeans with off-white beige lace around the holes ripped into them, she didn't look like the boss of anything, but Amelia knew that tone of voice. Their staff knew it, too. It was the one you didn't argue with.

Unless you were Angie's big sister, of course. She shook her head. "I had to send him away, Angie. I couldn't keep being with him, knowing I was hurting him."

"Again, his choice," she said, but Amelia shook her head again. "I know, which is what I told him, and he was the one who chose to walk out the door."

She'd done the right thing.

She'd just never expected the pain to be so debilitating. No matter what she did, she couldn't make it stop.

"This isn't good for the baby."

"You think I don't know that?" It was a constant worry, and why she was trying so damn hard to recover. To move on. To figure everything out. Find what would cure her.

"Craig and I are too different. We've both already learned the hard way that we can't be happy without being true to ourselves."

"But what if you're looking at the wrong truth?"

She shook her head again, trying desperately to stay above water so she didn't drown in her own shortcomings. Because pushing Craig away didn't feel like being true to herself, either. "I don't get it," she said, needing to understand. "How can truth be wrong?"

"You're focused on being like Mom, based on what you were like with Mike, and on a house, a kind of home, that isn't right for you."

"Yeah. I hurt you, and those I care most about, Angie. The only way I live with myself is to remain focused on that. To learn from the mistakes."

Angie sipped. Sitting upright, not even touching

her hand like she usually did, leaving Amelia feeling cut off. Adrift. Not that she blamed her sister.

"How much time have we spent together the past three months?"

The innocuous question came out of the blue. Confusing her. "A lot." Which had nothing to do with anything.

"How often have we talked?"

"All the time. Every day. Like always."

"Exactly."

"So?"

"So…you managed to have Craig in your life and still be there for me."

That was different. "We weren't a couple. I wasn't putting him first."

"I think you did. If you weren't putting him first, you wouldn't have ended things when you knew he was getting hurt."

She'd stop anything she could if she knew she was hurting someone else.

"Remember, I'm your sister and attached to your hip," Angie said. "I've been watching and I just wonder if maybe you and Craig have found a healthy relationship."

By being apart?

"It's not like either of us grew up with one to judge it by, or learn from," Angie said laconically, and then continued, "but you seem to know that he won't ask you to do anything that feels wrong to you. And you do the same for him. You don't rely on each other so much as you support each other. It's like you respect each other so much you don't want to do anything that's going to dishonor who either of you are, and what you need."

"There is that," she said. "But it's because we've always known we weren't a couple. Our lives aren't tied together. My choices don't have a direct effect on his life and vice versa."

"Really." More droll. "So your choice to use his sperm didn't affect him? Or all those weeks of hauling bikes around three times a week, scheduling things around the sacred exercise time, didn't affect his life? Because I have to tell you, it affected mine. I knew that unless there was an emergency I was not to ask you to do anything, or call you, during bike riding time."

"I'm sor—"

"Don't you dare apologize," Angie said. "This is what I'm getting at. Or kind of slowly coming to as I figure this all out. I don't think our relationship is the healthiest, either," she said, and Amelia started to spiral down so far she didn't recognize herself.

Angie still wasn't happy with her? With them?

Hers and Angie's was the one relationship she felt she had a grasp on and understood.

"It's not fair or right that I rely on my big sister for all of my support, that I expect you to always be the key relationship in my life."

Her face got cold. She stared, sure she was going to wake up from a nightmare. Angie took her hand, tears in her eyes. "I love our closeness. I love you. So much," she said. "I know you're always going to be a person I need to call when anything major happens in my life. I just need more. I need a life of my own. And I think you do, too."

Amelia saw the tears on her little sister's face and then she started really listening. Hearing Angie's words and digesting their meaning.

"I think that the way we grew up, in that house with a mean drunk and a mother who wouldn't or couldn't protect us, made us closer than a lot of siblings and I'm thankful for that," Angie continued. "I love it. I just think, as with anything, there are shadows to the bright sides. Maybe it made me, in particular, too reliant on you. I acted like I was your child, instead of Mom's, looking to you to be for me what she was not. I expected you to put me first…"

"You were a kid, Angie. We both were. I just happened to be older. Please don't think there's anything wrong with us. I love us. And you. I can't imagine a life without you."

Angie nodded, and cried a little more, too. "I know. Me, too. I'm not going anywhere, believe me. I just... Think about what I said. Maybe a bit of adjustment is in order. And maybe, if you see things a little differently, you'll be free to explore possibilities with Craig. Something that doesn't involve that house he's living in."

"He loves that house."

"A house is just a building. I have a feeling he might love you more."

He couldn't. His pain would be unbearable if he did. He'd already lost both Tricia and Gavin. And now her, and Isabella.

She couldn't breathe for a second as the weight of it all crashed in on her.

"He doesn't love me," she said. "You've never even met him, so how could you say that?"

"Because I see what he's done for you. And I don't just mean the bike riding. Or great sex." Angie grinned at that last part.

Amelia did, too, for a brief second.

"You've softened, sweetie. You've been happier in the past few months than I've ever seen you. Ever."

"Because of Isabella."

"I'm sure that's part of it, but look at you."

She glanced down. And though she knew Angie wasn't talking about her clothes, she couldn't look her sister in the eye. Wasn't ready to see what Angie had already seen. So she focused on the clothes, as though the answer would come in a softer way from the things that she'd lovingly created. She was wearing a pair of their high-end blue jeans from the new spring catalog, modified with a maternity waistband. A gift from Angie when they'd found out that Amelia was expecting. And a white, oversized cotton top that she'd picked up for a few bucks over the weekend because it was soft.

The top wasn't her style. But…it felt good. Better than any other shirt in her closet. Being with Craig felt better than anything she'd ever known in her life.

"What if you love him, Mel?"

She hoped she didn't. Hoped it would pass. But even if it didn't. "It wouldn't matter if I did. He wants to get married."

"Maybe you should think about that."

She shook her head. Adamantly. "I know I can't."

"Maybe you can."

"I can't live in that house."

"Maybe he'd move in a heartbeat if it meant he could be a family with you."

She shook her head. Again.

"I'm not saying he'd move. Or that you should marry him, Mel. I'm only saying that something's not right deep inside you. And it seemed perfectly right a week ago. Maybe it's time for you to reassess. Maybe you've learned from your mistakes with Mike, but you've let your fear that you can't trust yourself blind you to the fact that you've grown up. You've changed. You know your limits now. And yet, you could be letting them stop you from finding happiness."

"I'm happy with Isabella."

"And what is it going to do to her if she grows up with your entire happiness resting upon her? Can you imagine how hard it would be for her to ever leave home? Leave town? Follow her own dreams? If she loves you as much as I think she will, she'd be eaten up with guilt, leaving you alone…"

"Stop." She couldn't hear any more.

But she also couldn't deny that there was some truth in what her sister was saying.

"I don't want to love him."

"I think you do love him, though."

"I'm scared to death to love him."

"And right there…that's your truth."

* * *

On Wednesday, a week from the day he'd walked out of Amelia's life, Craig called her.

The contract he'd signed with the Parent Portal didn't give him the right to dial that number. The fact that he'd been her lover did. He'd had a long week. Wasn't in a real generous or patient frame of mind.

He'd been short with his PA, with his receptionist and with his closest friend. None of them deserved the treatment.

He'd apologized to all of them, one at a time. Had taken one out to dinner and given gift cards for dinner out to the other two.

"Craig?" She sounded breathless when she picked up the phone.

"I'd like a word with you, in person," he said. And then added, "At your convenience." He wasn't a complete boor.

He'd done a lot of thinking. He'd had no choice, being forced by his own petulance, to spend the majority of time with only himself and Talley for company.

That girl—she sure had a way of staring a guy down when she thought he needed to fix things.

"I'm free now," she said. "I'm still at the office. You want to come here?"

"Is your sister there?" He'd like to meet her on his way out the door.

"Yeah, but she has her own office."

"I'm on my way." Already in his car, he turned the wheel sharply, made a quick U-turn and sped up the street. Before he changed his mind and got all polite again.

Amelia was waiting for him at the back door of her suite in the plush, new, one-story complex.

"You look tired," he said, noting the darker skin around her eyes, the puffiness of her lids. The rest of her, what he could see of her in the baggy shirt, was just...good to be near.

"I am tired," she told him. "It's been a rough week."

She could have been referring to work, perhaps a computer crash or some other fashion-related crisis about which he would normally care a great deal. Because he knew she cared. And because her business was her livelihood.

He didn't care to be distracted at the moment. "Yes, it has been a rough week," he said, hands in the pockets of his navy pants as he walked into her office as though he'd been there before. He didn't look around. Didn't take in much. The smell was nice. The space roomy—with lots of floral patterns and bright colors. He adjusted his tie and shoved his hand right back into his pocket.

"I have some things to say," he said, reiterating what he'd told her in the car.

"Okay."

And there he was. At the point of no return. And couldn't remember, for a second, why he'd been so sure he had to reach that place. Until he glanced at the door he'd entered through and knew he'd be exiting it shortly.

"I love you," he said. "I am in love with you. Isabella is my daughter, biologically, but in my heart, too. I have no legal rights to her. I'm not asking for any, nor do I intend to do so, but no one has a right to dictate what's in my heart."

"I've realized some things. I've let fear..."

"I—"

He wasn't done yet. Couldn't let her distract him from finishing what he'd come to do. "I know you don't want to get married. I'm not asking you to. I just had to say what I have to say. This whole thing...it started out for good purpose, but my mistake was in continuing to see you when I knew I was falling in love. I fell in love with you not because of the baby you were carrying, but because you're the most fascinating, intriguing, frustrating woman I've ever known. That's when I should have left. I didn't. And now here we are, friends who can't be in touch because we took it too far. I'm sorry for that, too."

"I'm afraid to be a wife."

"I'm not asking you to be one," he said, finally looking her in the eye. Needing her to understand badly enough that he was willing to take the pain that came with connecting to her. "I'd never ask you to do something that is wrong for you, Amelia. Please don't misunderstand. At the same time, I can't go on understanding others and not speaking up on my own behalf. I get your situation, just like I got Tricia's. I respected her position, didn't want to pressure her, and so I never told her how deeply it affected me. Maybe if I had, if I'd explained more completely my concerns where fathering Gavin without legal protections was concerned, if I'd continued to speak them, something might have been different. Maybe not. I'm not here to try to convince you of anything. Or pressure you. I don't want a relationship that doesn't fit. In the long run it would be catastrophic. I just needed to say what I had to say. So that if you contact me in the future, and I hope you will, just for occasional updates if nothing else, everything is out in the open. We all know clearly where we stand."

"I'm afraid."

Their gazes were locked this time as she said the words. A sheen appeared in those expressive green-with-a-tint-of-gold eyes. Her lip trembled.

And his hands started to shake.

"I'm afraid, Craig. Afraid to spread myself too thin. To have to choose between a husband and child. Afraid I'll make the wrong choice. Like I did with Mike and Angie. I'm not saying I don't want to try, because I know I do...and I'm petrified I'll screw up..."

Was she giving him hope here?

"Angie wasn't your responsibility," he said, trying to adjust his thinking, just in case. Leaving a door open that he'd come to close. "She's your sister, not your daughter, and he, by all accounts, was a controlling, insecure creep." He wasn't holding anything back. There was just too much at stake.

"She looked to me to be the mother our mom couldn't be. We, uh, had a talk yesterday."

Shifting his weight back and forth between his heels and his toes, he adjusted his tie again. Loosened it a bit. Stood in that proverbial doorway, both feet in, but with the escape route open.

"So, you're afraid."

She nodded.

"But not necessarily opposed, morally, ethically or in your heart of hearts to give us a try?"

Biting her lower lip, she narrowed her eyes, but didn't turn away from him. "In my heart of hearts I'm so in love with you there is nothing else. I want to be your wife, Craig. That's my truth. But I'm still desperately afraid of that, too."

Through pursed lips, he watched her. Looked for signs of prevarication. Of uncertainty. Signs that she was saying what she thought he needed to hear. A sign that she was speaking out of need to tend to him, not from the truth in her heart. But there were none.

"Ask her to marry you already!"

Swinging around, Craig did a double take as a woman with a striking resemblance to Amelia threw back the office door that led into the suite. "You both are a piece of work." The woman, who was most clearly Angeline Grace, came into the room. "Both of you taking care of others to the point of not just grabbing for yourselves. Grab, for God's sake."

"Craig, I'd like you to meet my sister, Angie," Amelia said, still standing just as he'd left her.

He turned back to Amelia, leaving a beautiful woman behind him, but one who didn't shine at him as Amelia did.

"Amelia Grace, will you marry me?" he asked.

She nodded, biting her lip, blinking back tears.

He heard a little gulp behind him and turned to see Angeline crying, too, her hands clasped against her mouth.

"I know she comes as a package deal," he told Angie, as serious as he could be. "Isabella and you, too."

Angie sniffed. Kept her arms up and her hands on either side of her chin as she said, "And you're going to have to move," she told him. "She's the marrying kind, but some issues…"

"I'm fine living in a tepee if Amelia's there," he said, figuring he was getting his first taste of the rest of his life. He turned back to the woman who'd changed everything for him. "The house was a symbol of something," he said. "This week, being there alone, it was nothing but an empty reminder of what I didn't have. I've already met with a Realtor and put it on the market."

He heard the door close quietly behind them, and knew that dinner that night had to include Angie. Wanted it to include her. He'd taken her on.

They'd also need to call his parents. And he had another problem solved, too. A daughter-in-law and granddaughter were going to take care of the whole upcoming anniversary gig.

"But…you love that house, Craig. It's your home…and you're mine… I know that now."

"I found my home, my family, in your condominium, Amelia. And any other place you might ever need to live." He'd schedule times to run home to the condo during the day to put Talley out. And walk her instead of riding every night. Or they could walk her together. He probably wasn't going to be doing much bike riding anymore. Not for a little while, anyway. Until Isabella was old enough to sit in a child carrier on the back.

"I was thinking, maybe, we could move to the ground floor? Those homes have yard areas where my balcony is. That way Talley could have her doggy door…"

Sliding his hand beneath her hair, he looked at her. Just stood staring. A little slow to accept what his eyes were telling him. That when love arrived there were no problems too big to handle.

"I love you, Amelia Grace."

"I love you, too."

He kissed her then. Deeply. And she kissed him back. An honest, open kiss. One that promised more than just a moment.

One that promised a life.

* * * * *

Book One in The Parent Portal miniseries—
Having the Soldier's Baby—*is available now.*
And don't miss Book Three—
Her Motherhood Wish—
coming in April 2020 from
Harlequin Special Edition!

WE HOPE YOU ENJOYED
THIS BOOK FROM

HARLEQUIN
SPECIAL
EDITION

Believe in love. Overcome obstacles. Find happiness.

Relate to finding comfort and strength in the support of loved ones and enjoy the journey no matter what life throws your way.

6 NEW BOOKS AVAILABLE EVERY MONTH!

COMING NEXT MONTH FROM

H HARLEQUIN

SPECIAL EDITION

Available March 17, 2020

#2755 FORTUNE'S GREATEST RISK
The Fortunes of Texas: Rambling Rose • by Marie Ferrarella
Contractor Dillon Fortune wasn't always so cautious. But as a teenager, impulse led to an unexpected pregnancy and a daughter he was never allowed to know. Now he guards his heart against all advances. If only free-spirited spa manager Hailey Miller wasn't so hard to resist!

#2756 THE TEXAN TRIES AGAIN
Men of the West • by Stella Bagwell
Taggert O'Brien has had a rough few years, so when he gets an offer for the position of foreman at Three Rivers Ranch, he packs up and leaves Texas behind for Arizona. But he was not prepared for the effect Emily-Ann Broadmore—a barista at the local coffee shop—would have on him or his battered heart. Can he set aside his pain for a chance at lasting love?

#2757 WYOMING SPECIAL DELIVERY
Dawson Family Ranch • by Melissa Senate
Daisy Dawson has just been left at the altar. But it's her roadside delivery, assisted by a mysterious guest at her family's ranch, that changes her life. Harrison McCord believes *he* has a claim to the ranch and is determined to take it—but Daisy and her newborn baby boy have thrown a wrench in his plans for revenge.

#2758 HER MOTHERHOOD WISH
The Parent Portal • by Tara Taylor Quinn
After attorney Cassie Thompson finds her baby's health is at risk, she reluctantly contacts the sperm donor—only to find Woodrow Alexander is easily the kindest, most selfless man she's ever met. He's just a biological component, she keeps telling herself. He's *not* her child's real father or the husband of her dreams...right?

#2759 DATE OF A LIFETIME
The Taylor Triplets • by Lynne Marshall
It was just one date for philanthropist and single mom Eva DeLongpre's charity. And a PR opportunity for Mayor Joe Aguirre's reelection. Giving in to their mutual attraction was just a spontaneous, delicious one-off. But as the election turns ugly, Joe is forced to declare his intentions for Eva. When the votes are counted, she's hoping love wins in a landslide.

#2760 SOUTHERN CHARM & SECOND CHANCES
The Savannah Sisters • by Nancy Robards Thompson
Celebrity chef Liam Wright has come to Savannah to rebrand a local restaurant. And pastry chef Jane Clark couldn't be more appalled! The man who impulsively fired her from her New York City dream job—and turned her life upside down—is now on her turf. And if the restaurant is to succeed, Liam needs Jane's help navigating Savannah's quirky culture...and their feelings for each other.

YOU CAN FIND MORE INFORMATION ON UPCOMING HARLEQUIN TITLES, FREE EXCERPTS AND MORE AT HARLEQUIN.COM.

HSECNM0320

*Harrison McCord was sure he was the rightful owner
of the Dawson Family Ranch. And delivering Daisy
Dawson's baby on the side of the road was a mere
diversion. Still, when Daisy found out his intentions,
instead of pushing him away, she invited him in, figuring
he'd start to see her in a whole new light. But what if
she started seeing him that way, as well?*

*Read on for a sneak preview of the next
book in Melissa Senate's
Dawson Family Ranch miniseries,*
Wyoming Special Delivery.

Daisy went over to the bassinet and lifted out Tony,
cradling him against her. "Of course. There's lots
more video, but another time. The footage of what the
ranch looked like before Noah started rebuilding to the
day I helped put up the grand reopening banner—it's
amazing."

Harrison wasn't sure he wanted to see any of that. No,
he knew he didn't. This was all too much. "Well, I'll be
in touch about that tour."

*That's it. Keep it nice and impersonal. "Be in touch"
was a sure distance maker.*

She eyed him and lifted her chin. "Oh—I almost
forgot! I have a favor to ask, Harrison."

Gulp. How was he supposed to emotionally distance
himself by doing her a favor?

She smiled that dazzling smile. The one that drew him like nothing else could. "If you're not busy around five o'clock or so, I'd love your help in putting together the rocking cradle my brother Rex ordered for Tony. It arrived yesterday, and I tried to put it together, but it has directions a mile long that I can't make heads or tails of. Don't tell my brother Axel I said this—he's a wizard at GPS, maps and terrain—but give him instructions and he holds the paper upside down."

Ah. This was almost a relief. He'd put together the cradle alone. No chitchat. No old family movies. Just him, a set of instructions and five thousand various pieces of cradle. "I'm actually pretty handy. Sure, I can help you."

"Perfect," she said. "See you at fiveish."

A few minutes later, as he stood on the porch watching her walk back up the path, he had a feeling he was at a serious disadvantage in this deal.

Because the farther away she got, the more he wanted to chase after her and just keep talking. Which sent off serious warning bells. That Harrison might actually more than just like Daisy Dawson already—and it was only day one of the deal.